"*Just for the Night* is a witty, sensual contemporary romance that will have you quickly turning the pages to see what happens next."
—*Romance Junkies*

"*Just for the Night* is a terrific character-driven romance, well worth a spot on your 'must read' list."
—*Eye On Romance*

"Tawny Weber's newest release,
Breaking the Rules, is a thrilling story that will have readers laughing out loud at the surprising situations that arise throughout the story."
—*Romance Junkies*

"If you're looking for a great read that will warm you up on a cold night look no further!"
—*Night Owl Reviews* on *Breaking the Rules*

"*A Babe in Toyland* delivers a stunning performance that completely satisfies."
—*Noveltalk*

"*A Babe in Toyland* is absolutely hysterical sexy fun!...I was giggling the whole time."
—*Joyfully Reviewed*

"Great characters, an excellent story and heat enough to ignite the senses makes *Riding the Waves* an excellent read to lead us into September. Another fantastic tale from Tawny Weber!"
—*CataRomance*

Dear Reader,

I recognize a lot of myself in my heroine
Maya Black. She's stubborn, unflinchingly loyal and
a total daddy's girl. And like myself, she found her
perfect guy. Simon is not only sexy, but he's clever
enough to keep her guessing and smart enough to
accept her—family and all.

Sex, Lies and Midnight also features another
character who's very close to my heart—Dottie the
cat, who lives at the Furry Friends Animal Shelter.
You can check out Dottie, and all the other Blaze
Authors Pet Project pets, on the Blaze Authors
blog: http://blazeauthors.com. Please come by and
say hi! And if you're on the web, be sure to drop by
my website at www.tawnyweber.com. While you're
there, check out my members-only section with its
special contests, excerpts and other fun.

Happy New Year!

Tawny Weber

Tawny Weber

SEX, LIES AND MIDNIGHT

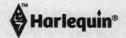

TORONTO NEW YORK LONDON
AMSTERDAM PARIS SYDNEY HAMBURG
STOCKHOLM ATHENS TOKYO MILAN MADRID
PRAGUE WARSAW BUDAPEST AUCKLAND

Recycling programs
for this product may
not exist in your area.

ISBN-13: 978-0-373-79664-9

SEX, LIES AND MIDNIGHT

Printed in U.S.A.

ABOUT THE AUTHOR

Tawny Weber is usually found dreaming up stories in her California home, surrounded by dogs, cats and kids. When she's not writing hot, spicy stories for the Harlequin Blaze line, she's shopping for the perfect pair of shoes or drooling over Johnny Depp pictures (when her husband isn't looking, of course). Come by and visit her on the web at www.tawnyweber.com or on Facebook at www.facebook.com/TawnyWeber.RomanceAuthor.

Books by Tawny Weber

HARLEQUIN BLAZE

To get the inside scoop on Harlequin Blaze and its talented writers, be sure to check out blazeauthors.com.

Don't miss any of our special offers. Write to us at the following address for information on our newest releases.

Harlequin Reader Service
U.S.: 3010 Walden Ave., P.O. Box 1325, Buffalo, NY 14269
Canadian: P.O. Box 609, Fort Erie, Ont. L2A 5X3

To my first ever hero.
Thank you for your acceptance,
your encouragement and for being
such a wonderful example for me.
You're amazing. I love you, Dad.

Prologue

"You must be pleased with yourself."

"Definitely pleased," Tobias Black agreed with the caller. "And a little surprised that our own sheriff turned out to be the dealer of sex drugs."

"The drug ring is broken but it doesn't end with him. Someone higher was pulling strings. Any idea who?"

Taking the phone off Speaker, Tobias lifted the handset to his ear, then stared at the glowing tip of his cigar and considered the question. A month ago, he'd chosen to bring the FBI in to help bust the drug ring specializing in a new-fangled form of Ecstasy that'd been blazing through his small town. His eldest son, Caleb, had helped the FBI bust that ring.

He'd brought the FBI in knowing than someone had more in mind that peddling sex drugs. Someone with a grudge against him. But as far as he was concerned, the FBI could butt out now. Tobias preferred to figure out who was trying to knife him in the spine himself. He was funny that way.

"No idea who was issuing Kendall's orders, but I'm not worried," Tobias lied smoothly. "It's nothing I can't handle."

"Even with the new sheriff in your corner, this time you just might be in over your head. My resources have uncovered yet more criminal activity and quite a few rumblings of something big coming soon."

Shit. He didn't need this. In his mind, the FBI had had a single purpose. To use their connections to bring his son home. That plan had worked, Caleb was now the acting sheriff, engaged to a pretty little thing in town, and slowly allowing Tobias to rebuild a bridge between them.

Right now, Tobias was busy setting into action goal number two. Better known as luring his daughter, Maya, back home. He didn't have time to keep playing these cop games.

He stared through the smoke at the awkwardly shaped ceramic bowl, glazed a brilliant red with fingerprints all along the edges. Every once in a while, he wondered if he was still smoking his daily cigar just for the joy of using the ashtray his five-year-old daughter had made. A dynamic, controlled man, he didn't consider overt sentiment a weakness. But he did consider not having more to be sentimental about a waste.

"I'm sure your associates at the FBI are looking at Kendall's associates and haven't given up on discovering who's behind it all," Tobias said. No longer having the taste for a relaxing cigar, he stubbed it out and stood to pace. "In the meantime, we'll handle things here in Black Oak. Caleb has years of experience with the DEA, and he'll make a fine sheriff. There's nothing to worry about here."

"That's not what I'm hearing," the man on the phone reminded him. "Someone is gunning for you. And instead of dealing with that, you're busy playing footsie with a woman young enough to be your daughter."

Tobias gave a wicked grin. "You make me sound like a dirty old lech, saying it that way."

"What else should you sound like?"

"A clever man who knows just which buttons to push?"

Eight years ago, Tobias had made a vital mistake. After

years of pulling cons on his own, of only working, occasionally, with his children, he'd taken on a partner.

Greta von Lautner.

It'd been the last straw for his volatile children.

Caleb had left to join the DEA, tired of his father's life of crime. Gabriel had accused his father of thinking with his penis, and walked out vowing to prove himself a better con than his old man had ever been.

And Maya? Tobias's sweet little angel had been heartbroken, not only at the change in dynamics, but at what she saw as being ousted from her place in her father's life. She'd tried to stick around, though. Then Greta had blown the con they were in the middle of; she'd left Maya vulnerable. Tobias had worked fast to clear the evidence and spring Maya from jail, but it'd been too late.

She'd walked out of that police department and his life in the same hour. Now, seven years later, it was time to reel her back.

"Those buttons you're pushing are trouble. Give me a good crime to solve any day over anything that involves women."

Tobias sighed, knowing he was treading a dangerous line.

"There's no other way. I want Maya home, and the only way she's going to return is if she thinks she's saving me from repeating a huge mistake."

"You're playing a dangerous game. You want to con your kids, do it after we've figured out who is trying to set you up."

"No game worth playing doesn't carry an element of danger," Tobias returned with a wicked laugh. "And the ball is already rolling. I can't stop it now."

"But you didn't plan for these stakes when you started. You just wanted your kids home. Now you're fighting for your reputation, your freedom and possibly your life."

Tobias looked out the window at the holiday lights twinkling merrily, making the view of Black Oak almost magical.

"If it reunites my family, even those stakes are worthwhile," he declared.

"You'd just better hope they aren't reuniting for your sentencing hearing." There was a pause, then a deep sigh. "Or if the rumblings I'm hearing are correct, at your funeral."

_**1**_

THERE WAS NOTHING like a short, glittery skirt, long legs encased in smoky stockings and spiked do-me heels to make a man sit up and take notice.

And Simon Barton considered it his duty to watch this particular woman currently shimmying her hips rhythmically on the dance floor. The investment firm's holiday party was in full swing, complete with barely dressed women, many soon-to-be-regretted-when-sober PDAs, an open bar and a lush buffet.

For a people watcher, this party was better than the circus, juggling clowns and—Simon noted one guy slipping his hand down the dress of the sloshed woman draped over his lap—a porno flick, all rolled into a single package.

But he only had eyes for one woman.

Not because she was gorgeous. Although she was.

Long black hair fell in curls almost to the tiny waist of a vivid green dress that had as much sparkle as her hips had personality. The fabric hugged a body made to bring grown men to their knees, long sleeves and a high neck giving the illusion of modesty at odds with the sexy placemat that passed for a skirt. Legs way too long for such a petite body were encased in smoke black stockings leading all the way down to a pair of strappy sandals so high, Simon could only wince.

The woman was fascinating.

Not because she seemed to have this knack for making herself invisible, despite her striking looks. Although she did. Every time one of, from what Simon could tell were the high muckety-mucks wandered past, she shifted. Unobtrusively placing another dancer, diner or chit-chatter between her and the higher-ups.

And not because she was a puzzle. Although, oh yeah, she was. One he was sure he'd solve. Sooner or later.

Because she was the key to his future.

He felt, rather than heard, his cell phone ring in the pocket of his slacks.

His gaze still locked on the overblown beauty on the dance floor, Simon pulled out his phone. He glanced at the readout, grimaced, then stepped into a quiet corner where his view was unimpeded, but the sound was muted.

"Barton."

"I thought you were on assignment."

"I wrapped it up. Now I'm on personal time."

"Watching Maya Black is a personal thing for you?"

Christ. Did Hunter have eyes everywhere? Simon gave an infinitesimal wince, his eyes still on those lush hips encased in holiday green. "A man would have to be three-times dead not to have a personal reaction to watching a woman like her."

"How'd you find her?"

"I'm a trained FBI agent," Simon said sardonically. "An assumed name is a piece of cake."

"You hacked her file?" Hunter's words were matter-of-fact.

Simon shifted his eyes off the sweetly swaying hips to inspect his fingernails. "Would I do that?"

"In a heartbeat."

Simon grinned.

Whether he knew it or not, Hunter was Simon's mentor. The man whose career he'd used as a template for his own. Simon wanted nothing more than to climb the same ladders and spark the same attention. The Deputy Director was considered the elite of the elite. A man with a reputation for making the rules work for him, even as he worked around them. Assignment to Hunter's department was Simon's Holy Grail. There he'd rise through the ranks at least twice as fast as anywhere else. But Hunter's team was so exclusive, he only brought in major players. Agents who'd made huge busts.

Busts like the Black case. Simon's gaze wandered back to the tempting sway of Maya Black's hips. Since it was totally inappropriate to lust after a suspect, he tried to convince his body that the surge of energy he felt at the sight of her was because she was his ticket to a major promotion.

"Why are *you* watching her?" he challenged, tossing the ball back in Hunter's court.

"Who says I am? I might be watching you."

Simon's laugh garnered more than one appreciative female glance. Not unusual. He got a lot of looks from ladies. Sometimes he used the advantages his tall, well-built golden-boy looks offered. Other times he ignored them.

This time, he nodded at a couple of them, but shifted his weight, making it clear he wasn't looking for more. He might not be on the job, per se, but this was all business.

"Maya Black isn't a person of interest. You're out of bounds."

Simon shrugged that off. He figured boundaries were a fluid thing. He only paid attention to the ones that served him.

"She's got a record," he pointed out.

"Arrest, no conviction."

"She was guilty."

"We don't know that. No," Hunter interrupted before Simon could haul out his well-worn argument, "we don't. We have conjecture, speculation and a whole lot of circumstantial supposition."

What they had were sloppy agents who had obviously been incompetent. Maya Black had been busted for computer invasion, breaking into the files of a well-placed businessman with a bad reputation. The case should have been open and shut, but the arresting officers had neglected to confiscate all of the computers on site when they'd brought her in. Within hours, the evidence had disappeared, the arrest compromised. Maya Black released.

Simon shook his head in disgust.

"She was running a Ponzi con with her old man and bungled it. If the agent in charge had been patient, he'd have had a solid case."

"That's your opinion," Hunter said, his tone one degree colder than before. It took Simon a heartbeat to remember that the agent in charge of the Black case was Hunter's father.

"It doesn't matter. I'm not here on official business. I'm just here, checking out the view," he hedged, returning to the reason for Hunter's call.

"You're stepping on dangerous ground," Hunter warned.

"I live for danger." That wasn't the official FBI motto, but Simon had seen enough of it in his nine years with the agency that he figured he had the right to use it as an excuse.

"Don't die for it," Hunter responded in typical fashion before hanging up.

Simon grinned. You had to like the guy. He was crazy smart, scary intuitive and could kick some serious ass, too. And he didn't hold the reins too tight on his agents. Which was why Simon wasn't too worried about stepping outside the lines in this matter. Hunter was more about results than he was about micromanaging. Yet another reason Simon wanted that transfer. Working with the elite would let him hone his skills, and fast track him toward his own shot at Deputy Director.

Something he'd dreamed of since he was a kid. That dream had been the impetus to haul himself out of the dregs that was his childhood. Not just to survive, but to thrive. Making that dream come true would prove, not just to him, but to everyone who'd ever doubted him, that he was more than the loser with no future.

Which brought him back to the voluptuous delight laughing and doing the twist by the twinkling lights of the ten-foot Christmas tree. She was hot. She was sexy. And she was his ticket. Not to the next rung on the ladder, but to jumping up three or four rungs at once.

Tobias Black was a legend. Reputed con artist who'd done more jobs than a hooker in the financial district at lunchtime. He was slick, quick and according to most, untouchable. Intel had him retiring to go straight about five years back, but the statute of limitations wasn't up on all of his crimes yet. Simon knew that busting the old man, where so many had failed over the years, would be a guarantee of fame, accolades and a corner office in FBI headquarters, D.C.

He hadn't figured out how, yet. But he was pretty sure the guy's only daughter would be his key. He just had to wait for the right break. That he'd already been waiting for two years, checking in on Maya from time to time, didn't bother him. Patience was a weapon he'd honed to a razor-sharp edge.

Every few months he laid over in San Francisco to do a little recon and see what she was up to. Sooner or later, she'd get edgy and tire of this straight game she was playing.

Sooner or later, she'd give him the opening he needed.

Then he'd have her.

And his future would be set.

"WHEW, I NEED A BREAK." Maya DeLongue slid the fingers of both hands into her hair and lifted it, trying to get some cool air on the back of her neck. "It's crazy hot in here. Can we get a drink?"

"Sure, sugar." Her date wrapped his hand around her waist, pulling her close. Always wary of public displays of affection that might call attention to her, Maya shifted, taking Dave's hand off her waist and making a show of holding it instead as he led her from the dance floor.

Braverment Investments knew how to show their employees a good time. Plenty of alcohol flowing, just enough food to blunt the worst of the booze overload and music loud enough to prevent the employees from actually having to socialize. It was a hit.

A tension headache brewing, Maya already regretted coming.

She'd spent the last three years trying to be average in her version of the witness protection program, or in her case, the criminal protection program. Her position in IT at Braverment was perfect for her. It paid enough to keep her in the style her tastes required, in a company large enough to let her hide in plain sight. But the powers-that-be probably wouldn't be too big on hiring a gal who'd spent her formative years specializing in computer hacking.

But average was lonely.

So she'd promised herself that this season she was going to quit hiding away. She had to be able to hide her true identity and have a fun, average life at the same time. So she'd forced herself to shimmy into a little green holiday dress and play the part of a social butterfly.

Sighing, she shifted in her Jimmy Choos and stepped through the wide glass doors onto the rooftop balcony. The cold December night wrapped around her body, making her shiver. The view of the fog-shrouded Golden Gate Bridge more than made up for the chilly weather, though.

"Hey, Carly," she greeted when they reached one of the many tables scattered under the night sky. "Can we join you?"

Maya wasn't especially fond of the other woman, another assistant at the investment firm they both worked for. The busty blonde was ambitious, backstabbing and didn't play well with the other girls. But Maya knew she had to play nice with people like Carly to keep their knives as far away from her own back as possible.

"Sure," the blonde agreed, puffing on her cigarette and checking Dave out before waving a hand to indicate the empty chairs.

"Can I get you ladies drinks?" Dave offered.

"Martini," Carly agreed instantly.

"I'll stick with water," Maya said. Seeing their looks, she excused, "I'm a little dehydrated from all the dancing."

The truth was, she didn't drink alcohol. Ever. But neither did she like explaining herself, so she kept that little fact private.

She folded herself into one of the chairs, enjoying the way Dave's gaze roamed over her legs. In her quest for a normal, average life, she'd finally given herself permission to date a guy she might have a future with. Sure, this was only their third date, but she had high hopes for Dave. He was nice.

"A martini and a water," Dave said, his eyes glommed on to her thighs. "Got it."

With a grin and a wink, he turned on his heel and hurried back into the party. Maya sighed. It was pretty obvious that someone thought he was getting lucky tonight.

"He's hot. Are you two serious?" Carly asked.

Maya glanced at the blonde before her gaze followed the path Dave had taken. He *was* hot. Sorta. Sorta-tall, sorta-dark, sorta-handsome. Sure, that sexy bad-boy edge that usu-

ally drew her was missing. But that was the point. That made
him safe, which was priority number one.

"We're having fun," she said, sidestepping the question.
"How about you? Are you here with someone?"

They spent the next few minutes exchanging desultory
chit chat. Maya's gaze wandered, noting the twinkling lights
framing the balcony, the few occupied tables and the noted
lack of excitement she was feeling.

She'd been doing this *normal life* thing for three years now.
In part, to prove she could. But mostly because she'd never
had normal growing up. Like some kids craved the exotic,
she'd craved average.

But she'd come to realize that average, after a while, was
pretty damned boring. Hence Dave. And he was a nice guy.
She just didn't feel any real excitement, any wildly hot energy
between them.

Maybe it was time to move on?

She was still mulling that idea, and just what it would
mean to her life, when Dave returned with the drinks. She
listened to him and Carly chat and wondered what it was like
to be that carefree. For a girl who'd been calculating the odds
since her toddler years, the concept was totally foreign.

"Maya, you don't mind if I borrow your friend for a dance
or two?" Carly asked, slinking to her feet in a move worthy
of the most sinuous snake in the jungle.

Maya smirked when she saw the slight bulge of Dave's
eyes as he got the full impact of Carly's double Ds. She
couldn't blame him. The view was mesmerizing, in a train-
wreck kind of way.

"Sure," she said. Then she added, "But just a couple
dances. I expect him back in the same shape you're borrow-
ing him."

Dave laughed like a giddy schoolboy, but Carly caught the
message. Her vamp smile dimmed a notch, then she nodded

before leading Dave away. As they entered the room, though, Maya saw the other woman's hand slip over Dave's ass.

She should be jealous. Pissed, even. But she wasn't. Why not? He was a nice guy. And he fit perfectly into her average life. Her nice, average boyfriend. Someone to ease her loneliness. Maya sighed, wishing the cool night air would clear her head of all the confusing thoughts.

She stood to walk toward the balcony wall and get a better view of the Golden Gate, but accidentally knocked her water bottle off the table as she rose.

It spun across the outdoor carpet toward the shadows. She hurried over to grab it just as it rolled to a stop at a pair of feet clad in high-end cowboy boots.

Maya sighed. A cowboy in California? *Oh, please.*

Keeping her eye roll to herself, she stopped a foot away and checked out the rest of the wild west show. Her mental sneer shifted as her gaze climbed up long, long jeans-clad legs, a leather belt around a narrow waist and a chest that begged to be nuzzled. The collar of a dark green shirt was opened, his jacket looked pricey and…she let her gaze finish the climb.

And felt the earth shift just a little.

Oh, baby, he was gorgeous.

A square jaw and slashing cheekbones were the perfect frame for a face that could sell magazines, cars and women's souls. Long-lashed eyes echoed the green of his shirt, his lips were kissably full and the only thing keeping him from being a pretty boy was a scar, high on his cheekbone.

One side of his mouth quirked in amusement at her inspection as he bent down to grab the bottle.

"Yours?" he asked, his voice declaring his right to wear those thousand-dollar cowboy boots. Cultured, rich and definitely Southern.

"Thank you," Maya murmured, taking the water. Her brow knit. "Have we met?"

Her face heated and wished she could take back the words. *Oh, man, what a cliché.* She'd have done just as well to offer to strip him naked and dance around his body like a stripper's pole.

Since she couldn't erase the words, instead she gave a short laugh and shook her head. "I know, it sounds like a cheesy pickup line. But I swear, I've seen you before."

Gifted with a near-photographic memory, she never forgot numbers and she never forgot a face. The former made her a prized assistant among the investment bankers in her department. The latter kept her past from tripping her up.

The problem was, she couldn't remember exactly who he was. She'd seen him a few times around Braverment events, so he must work for the company in some form or another. Probably one of their out-of-state branches.

"I'd remember if we had," he returned with a smile that did wicked things to her libido.

"My mistake," she excused, irritated to hear how breathless the words sounded. She cleared her throat and plastered on her brightest smile. "Are you with Braverment?"

"No. Old man Braverment is a friend of the family and he suggested I drop in. I'm actually here looking for capital. A few investors interested in a new app platform to integrate social media." He flashed her a smile so wicked with charisma she figured he raked in investments like crazy.

Amazing. Even boring investment talk sounded sexy in that delicious accent. Pretending her knees weren't wobbling, she asked, "Are you enjoying the party?"

"I appreciate the view," he returned. His voice was as sexy as his face. Husky and low, making her think of magnolia blossoms and mint juleps, silk sheets and naked bodies. Maya wished it were a little cooler on the patio, since her body was feeling very, very hot.

He nodded toward the doors leading to the Christmas festivities, and asked, "How about you? Are you having a good time?"

The tiny hairs on the back of Maya's neck stood up. She didn't know why. Other than being way too sexy for his own good, he shouldn't make her feel threatened. Should he? She'd seen him before so he was legit, and he was gorgeous.

It was probably the gorgeous part that was setting off her warning signals. To say nothing of making her body go into sexual hyperdrive.

Once or twice, she'd thought she could have her cake and eat it, too. That she could be average and still give in to the wild, passionate side of her nature. But she'd been burned, badly. So she avoided all guys who tripped her passion meter. It'd only been a few months ago that she'd even felt safe dating a mellow, safe guy like Dave.

But this guy would not only trip the meter, he'd send it spinning out of control. Because he'd demand everything. He'd plumb the depths of passion, he'd discover untapped levels of sensuality that Maya was pretty sure were hiding beneath the surface. He had the potential to drive her straight over the edge to crazy.

But average girls who didn't like to attract attention didn't do crazy.

"I am enjoying the party, thanks," she responded, shifting her tone from friendly to distant. Then she gestured toward the door. "And I should be getting back to the dance floor. They're playing my favorite song."

"Merry Christmas," he called as she walked away.

Maya glanced back. Yes, his eyes were glued to her. She swallowed hard, then offered a quick smile. "Merry merry to you, too," she said.

Whew. She bypassed the dance floor to find the ladies' room instead. She needed cold water. Or better yet, an ice bath.

"IT WAS A GREAT EVENING, Dave, thanks so much for going to the party with me," Maya said.

"We don't have to end the fun yet," he said, rubbing his hands up and down her arms in a gentle caress. "I'm still in the party mood."

To prove his point, he zoomed in with an enthusiastic kiss. Maya sighed, leaning in to enjoy herself. This was nice, she realized. But—she pulled away with a sigh—not exciting.

What was wrong with her?

"I'd invite you in, but my roommate is waiting up," she excused.

With that, and a quick little finger wave, she slipped through her front door, threw the lock and leaned back against it with a heavy sigh. "I hate dating."

"It is a necessary evil," Tiffany declared, looking all comfy in her Snuggie on the couch. Her engagement ring flashed bright in the light of the TV, declaring that while she respected the dating evil, it wasn't a game she had to play any longer.

Which was just one of the many reasons Maya had chosen her as a roommate. She was sweet and fun and tidy. She was totally involved in her own life, so didn't have a lot of spare time to poke into Maya's. And best of all, she was temporary, without that being an apparent requirement.

She was also Maya's fifth roommate in the three years she'd owned the sweet Victorian here in San Francisco. The few people at Braverment who knew her well enough to be aware of her living arrangements teased her about her bad luck with roommate turnover. Maya always played up her faux despair, secretly thrilled at how well it all worked in her favor. After all, she hated living alone, but knew that a real long-term roommate would mean an element of intimacy she couldn't handle.

So, like everything else in her life, she kept her shared-living arrangements short and sweet. And more importantly, totally superficial.

"How was your night?" Maya asked as she shrugged out of her black velvet opera coat and hung it in the hall armoire. "TV, ice cream and a stack of bridal magazines? It looks like a good time to me."

"Throw in a honey-oatmeal facial and call me a wild woman," Tiffany joked.

Maya grinned, bending down to pry her darling strappy sandals off her dance-swollen feet. "You are one crazy gal."

"You had a phone call."

Maya's brows shot up. How weird. Usually, if someone wanted to reach her they called her cell. The only reason she even had a landline was for internet and to give pesky tele-marketers someplace to call.

"A sexy sounding guy, said his name was Caleb and that he'd get a hold of you later."

Missing a step, Maya stumbled over her bare feet, her precious Jimmy Choos flying into the wall. She reached out to keep herself from following and took a mandatory deep breath to try and gather her thoughts.

By any standard, Maya had had an unconventional up-bringing. Motherless by a year old, she'd never been a sweet little girl in the traditional sense. Instead, she'd learned the art of the three-card monte before she'd learned to read. By four, she'd learned to call up crocodile tears on command, the first time to keep her father from being arrested. She had amassed enough through computer hacking to pay her own tuition to Yale before she'd graduated high school.

So it was rare for her to be shocked.

"Caleb called?" she repeated faintly.

"You okay?" Tiffany asked, swinging her feet off the couch, concern clear on her face. "What's wrong? Is he an ex-boyfriend? A bad guy? Should I call Mark?"

That made Maya smile. Mark was Tiffany's fiancé—a bespeckled orthodontist who bowled on weekends—and she definitely saw him through the eyes of love. The idea of his sweet self coming up against the likes of six-foot-two, muscle-bound Caleb Black, the baddest of the bad Black boys, was a little funny.

Scary funny, but still enough to make her want to giggle.

"No," she said, gathering her scattered composure. "No, that's okay. Caleb isn't any kind of threat."

At least, not unless he mistakenly suspected her of suddenly having a yen to deal drugs. Her big brother was a badass DEA agent, usually so far undercover he probably didn't even remember her existence. So why was he calling her? And on the house phone? The house, like the phone and everything else she had here in California, was under the name of Maya DeLongue. So how had he tracked her down?

And why? Panic shot through her, making her heart race and her ears ring. Worried sick, her mind spun from one horrible scenario to the next. In the half-dozen times she'd heard from her brother since she'd left home seven years previous, he'd always called her cell. Why would he call the house?

Was he hurt? Had something happened to Dad? To their brother, Gabriel?

"Did he say when he'd be calling back?" she asked, trying not to sound like she was going to cry. Her dad was indestructible. Superman. He had to be okay. He just had to.

"No," Tiffany said, pushing a strand of toast-brown hair off her worry-creased forehead.

"Caller ID?"

"Unknown caller."

Maya cursed softly. Tiffany's frown deepened and she started chewing on her thumbnail. "I'm sorry. Should I have pushed him for more information? I didn't want to give him your cell number, you know, just in case he was a crazy or something."

That made her laugh. Caleb, crazy? Oh, yeah, definitely. Maya took a deep breath and shoved both hands through her heavy curls. This was ridiculous. She was overreacting. Christmas was in two weeks. He was probably just calling to wish her a happy holiday, or to see if she'd heard any news of their father.

Everyone was okay.

They had to be.

Because while she might have cut her family so far out of her life that she denied their very existence, didn't use their name and hadn't seen any of them in six years, they were still the most important thing in her entire world.

And, she vowed, if everybody was okay, she was going to kick Caleb's ass for giving her such a scare.

2

MAYA SHOT STRAIGHT UP OFF her pillow, her vision obscured by a tangle of hair as she tried to figure out what had woke her.

The chirping phone answered her question.

"Hello?" she asked in a sleep-roughened tone. She'd gone to bed in the wee hours after midnight, then tossed and turned while worrying until almost five. She squinted through the dim light, noting that it was now eight. Yuck.

"Morning, Maya. How was the party?"

Her smile spread so big she was sure her ears were creasing. He sounded good. Calm, happy even. Not the tone of a man about to share bad news.

"Caleb, you brat. How'd you find me?"

"You're kidding, right?"

Maya rolled her eyes. "The house isn't in my name. Shouldn't that slow your kind down a little?"

"That's child's play for my kind."

"So what's the deal? You lost my cell number and needed to prove you're not a child?"

"What? A big brother can't call his little sister on Christmas?"

"Christmas isn't for two weeks, you called last night and

I had my yearly call from you back in July. Seriously, what's going on?"

Not that Maya cared. She adored her big brother, so any reason to hear from him, barring injury or bad news, was good by her.

Almost giddy with delight, she plumped one of her half-dozen pillows behind her and pulled the silk sheet high over her Garfield T-shirt. These days Caleb was her only connection with her family. And he made that connection very rarely. So this was a treat to be savored.

Their middle brother, Gabriel, was like a ghost. He flitted in and out at will to remind them that he existed, but was rarely heard from and even more rarely seen. Unlike Caleb, who flitted because he was undercover DEA, nobody knew what Gabriel did. But his disdain for law enforcement was so deeply entrenched, Maya knew he wasn't undercover anything. *Unless it was under some woman's covers,* she thought with a grin.

Their father, on the other hand, was easy to find. Ensconced in Black Oak, California, he ruled the little town at the base of the Santa Cruz Mountains like a benevolent despot. He had no place in the town government, he ran a custom motorcycle shop instead of a bank or big business and he had a hazy history other than being a descendant of the town's founder. But he was still the man in charge, and everyone in Black Oak knew it.

Dynamic, charming and ruthless, Tobias Black was a force to be reckoned with.

Her smile faded, a little tug of pain aching in her chest.

As she settled back in preparation for the big news, Dottie, the cat who'd adopted her eight months before, jumped up on the bed. She curled around a couple times, making the down comforter puff before she settled on Maya's stomach with a purring sort of sigh.

"What's the big deal that inspired a holiday phone call?" Maya prodded as she rubbed the cat's chin. The adorable black-and-white face lifted for better scratching access.

"I'm back in Black Oak," Caleb told her.

Maya's smile dropped away and her fingers stilled. Her stomach jumped before taking a slow, swirling dive down to her bare toes. The room tilted and her brain scrambled. Was this some kind of code? Was Caleb being held prisoner by a drug-crazed lunatic and this was his goodbye call? Was there a hint in his words that she was supposed to use to save him?

"Quit hyperventilating," he chided, as if he were reading her mind. "I'm here by choice. Well, now I am. I came back as a favor to a friend and sort of got hooked."

She wanted to ask if he'd seen their father. But she knew he had. Nobody came through town without Tobias knowing, and he wouldn't let Caleb come and go without a confrontation.

She wanted to ask how Dad was. How he looked and if he'd aged. Was he still pining after that horrible bitch, Greta? Or had he finally accepted the idiocy of falling for a woman so fake she'd have smiled and batted her false lashes while she shivved him in his sleep?

Did he miss his daughter? Even a little?

Her stomach churning, Maya twisted her sheet between her fingers, the slick fabric bunching in puffs as she thought of seeing her dad again. How did Caleb feel about it?

Before she could ask, hell, before she could even figure out exactly what question to ask, Caleb continued.

"I'm engaged. To, you know, get married."

Shock slammed through Maya. She made a squeaking sound. Dottie rolled onto her back, batting at Maya like she was looking for the rubber mouse that'd made that noise. Before Maya could come up with a response, before she could think to ask who'd be crazy enough, or amazing enough, to capture her big brother's heart, he continued.

"And I'm moving back permanently."

Her next squeak was a pitch higher. Moving? Back? No way. Usually lightning-fast, her brain struggled to accept what he was saying. Dottie—apparently deciding that if it wasn't a toy making the noise, she wasn't interested—padded to the foot of the bed where she curled around herself in a ball of black and white fur.

"I can't believe…"

"There's more."

More? What more? Her big, bad brother, the man who avoided real life to the point that he spent most of his pretending to be other people, was tying himself to another person—and their hometown—for the rest of his life?

Her head spinning like she was on an amusement park ride, Maya made a noise for him to continue.

"I've taken on the temporary post of Sheriff."

Maya couldn't even squeak this time because her jaw had dropped in shock. She pressed her hand to her churning stomach, wondering if this particular ride was going to make her throw up.

"Maya?"

Staring blindly at her rich purple bedroom wall, she gave a humming sort of response.

"Maya? C'mon. Say something."

She opened her mouth to respond, then had to swallow. She cleared her throat, pulled the phone away to check the caller ID, which claimed Unknown, and shook her head again.

"My little sister—the chatterbox of North America—with nothing to say?"

"Fine," she snapped, hating that nickname. She'd worked hard all her life to control her chattering impulses and Caleb knew it. "Who are you and what have you done with my real brother?"

His laugh was rich and warm, coming through the phone and wrapping around her like a brotherly hug.

"It's a good thing. It's all good." He sounded... Maya squinted in the morning light, trying to figure it out. He sounded content. Why the hell would he want to be content?

"I wanted to tell you and..." He trailed off, sounding a little unsure for the first time since she'd spied on him while he asked the head cheerleader on a date. If Maya recalled correctly, Caleb had been fourteen to the cheerleader's seventeen. And he'd tied Maya to a kitchen chair the night he'd gone on the date to keep her from following.

She wondered if he ever found out that Gabriel had freed her so they could both spy on him, then had covered her eyes and hauled her back home when it appeared that big brother was going to score.

Was it any wonder she couldn't settle for a guy? None could ever live up to the men in her family.

"And, what?" she prodded, not sure she was ready to hear it but figuring he needed to share. Probably something sappy and sentimental about their father. Begging her to come home, to reconcile. "You've already sent me into a state of absolute shock. Believe me, big brother, there isn't much left you can say to top you're back home, engaged to a real woman and leaving the DEA to be a small-town sheriff news."

But her heart pounded anyway. Maya shoved a hand through her hair, wincing when she hit sleep-roughened snarls.

Overcome, she threw the covers back, not realizing until she heard an angry meow that she'd buried the cat in down and silk. She flipped the covers off Dottie and stormed out of her room toward the kitchen. She needed a drink.

"Well, here's the thing. I'm hoping you'll come home. Just to visit. I know you have no reason to want to see Dad, or anyone in Black Oak. But I hope you'll consider it. Pandora's mom is throwing a party. Some big to-do to celebrate our engagement. I don't want it. Pandora doesn't want it, but Cassiopeia is insisting and Dad's backing her."

Conflicted over the idea of going home—of seeing her family for the first time in years—Maya paused in the act of squeezing the chocolate syrup into a tall glass of full-fat milk to frown. "Cassiopeia? The psychic?"

Caleb's sigh was so loud she was surprised it didn't ruffle her hair through the phone.

"Is your fiancée woo-woo, too?" Maya teased. Then, realizing her glass was now half chocolate to half milk, she quickly uprighted the squeeze bottle and closed the lid. She considered the glass of sugar-overload, then considered this phone call and grabbed a spoon to stir.

"Pandora's more a student of human nature with woo-woo overtones," he said. Her glass halfway to her lips, Maya lowered it and sighed as a wave of happiness enveloped her. He sounded so in love. Not gooey, but just really happy and filled with a joy she'd never thought her big, tough brother could feel.

"So, you know, I get it if you don't want to come back for the party. I don't blame you and honestly don't know if I'd come back if the situation was reversed. But I wanted to tell you about it."

Blinking fast to keep the tears at bay, Maya set her glass back on the counter, untouched. No point ruining fabulously chocolate milk with salt.

"You'd have come back," she said quietly. "A chance to play big brother, flex those muscles and boss me around a little? You'd have done it in a heartbeat."

He laughed, but didn't deny her words. Because for all that

Caleb had spent a whole bunch of years lying for a living, he was a painfully honest man.

And he was her big brother. Getting married. Maya grabbed the glass and took a big gulp, wiping her mouth with the back of her hand.

"Is Gabriel coming?" she hedged.

"Can't reach him. You know how it is, he's probably in the middle of some big scam and flying under the radar."

Unlike Caleb, who'd taken the complete opposite route as their con-artist father and gone into law enforcement, and Maya, who tried to pretend her father and his criminal habits didn't exist, Gabriel embraced his heritage. She was pretty sure he was determined to outdo their father's rep before he was thirty.

"Look, you're still pissed at Dad," Caleb said quietly.

Maya winced, wishing like crazy he'd be a typical guy and avoid the tough discussion.

"Actually, I am, too. But if you can't get past it, I'll understand. Pandora and I will take a weekend and come up to San Francisco so you can meet. No pressure, you do what you feel's right."

With that and a murmured goodbye, he was gone.

And her world was effectively turned upside down.

"So what d'ya say we skip the big parties and spend New Year's together at my place?" Dave was saying in a continuation of his campaign to take their relationship to the next level. "The two of us, a bottle of wine, a little fun."

Maya's smile was stiff enough to hurt her face. She was having major second thoughts about Dave. Sure, he was a nice guy. A perfect fit for her average life. Sure, he didn't make her heart race or her body melt. But racing and melting probably weren't average. But was it fair to lead him on if she really wasn't interested?

Ever since Caleb had called three days ago, she'd felt like this average life was suffocating her. All the more reason not to go home. Who knew what craziness she'd crave once she was exposed to the extravagant personalities that were her family.

"Well?" Dave prompted. "Are you going to be my New Year's date?"

What did she do? Choose average but boring? Or go back to her lonely life, hiding away in her house and staying away from any real relationship? Before she could decide, her cell phone rang. A little ashamed at how grateful she was to hear the bluesy tone, Maya offered an apologetic smile, then glanced at the readout. Shocked, her hand trembled just a little as she lifted it for a better look.

Lilah Gomez? Her best friend from high school? The lying, cheating slut who'd stolen Maya's boyfriend?

How had she gotten Maya's number? What the hell was she doing calling?

And why wasn't the past staying nicely tucked away like it was supposed to?

She debated ignoring it. She had nothing to say to the woman. Then she recalled Caleb's news about home. And her innate curiosity flared, making it impossible for her to resist.

"Excuse me," she murmured to Dave, giving him a smile with enough charm to make him preen. "I have to take this."

She slid out of the booth, hurrying through the brightly lit restaurant with its loud lunchtime crowd. She waited until she reached the garden enclosure just outside the restaurant before answering. "Hello?"

"Maya! Hi there. It's me, Lilah. You know, from the good old days?"

"Is that how you remember them?" Maya mused aloud.

Lilah's giggle was even more irritating than it'd been in the good old days.

"Your dad gave me your number. He's hoping you'll come home for the New Year's Eve engagement party. I hope you do. I mean, can you believe Caleb is getting married? She's so not worthy of a hottie like your brother. Yowza did he grow up into one delish hunk. And when he finally comes back to town, what does Pandora do? Grabs him up before anyone else gets a shot."

Anyone else, meaning Lilah.

"Why, exactly, are you calling? You know, after eight years of absolutely no contact?" Maya wasn't surprised that her father was keeping tabs on her. That was typical. But that he'd share anything with Lilah was a shock.

"I told you, I wanted to see if you were coming back for the engagement party. We have so much to catch up on. I want to hear all about your life, and I know you're dying to hear about mine," she said. Then, clearly not wanting Maya to die of curiosity, she started filling her in on the past eight years.

Tuning her out while she tried to figure out the angle Lilah was playing, Maya's eyes swept the restaurant. Dave was happily texting away, sneaking bites of her slice of chocolate cake.

Her eyes caught on another man at the other end of the garden. She recognized the sexily tousled sun-streaked hair and wide, do-me-baby shoulders. Desire did a slow, loopy swirl deep in her belly. Was that the same gorgeous Southern stud she'd encountered at the company party? Or was she just imagining a resemblance because she hadn't been able to stop thinking about the man?

"So, you know, I'm hoping it'll be a double celebration," Lilah was babbling.

"Sorry, what?" Maya asked, standing on tiptoes and craning her neck around the jungle of plants to see if it really was him. Yes, the man was off-limits due to his gorgeousness, his sexual magnetism and the fact that she was pretty sure she couldn't be in proximity to him for more than forty-five minutes and not jump his bones. A bad idea for a woman trying to contain her wilder impulses. But still… She had the right to enjoy the view.

"Double engagement," Lilah clarified, her words syrup sweet. "Caleb and Pandora. Me and Tobias. You know, your father."

Maya's jaw dropped. So did her feet as she fell from her tiptoes and almost landed on her butt. Knees like jelly, she reached out to grab the wall.

"No," she breathed.

"Oh, yes," Lilah said, her delight reaching through the line like a slap to Maya's face.

"No," she blurted out. "My father wouldn't do that."

He couldn't. Hadn't he learned anything from Greta the Grinch? The woman had used him, had tried to ruin him. She'd destroyed his life. Through her little hacking habit, Maya had kept track of Greta, finding comfort in the fact that her father had ended things with the bitch a few months after Maya had left home.

And now he was seeing Lilah Gomez? Had he fallen into senility? What the hell was wrong with the man?

"Poor Maya. I promise, I won't make you call me momma," Lilah said with a giggle. "But this will be so fun, won't it? Your dad, he's just so dreamy. And rich, of course. I love the power he holds over the town, too. That's so sexy in a man, don't you think?"

The only thing Maya thought was that she might be sick.

"He'd have to be crazy to go down this path again," she muttered. Was he trying to ruin his life again?

"Crazy in love. I mean, he hasn't asked yet," Lilah acknowledged reasonably. But Maya knew her well enough to recognize the gleeful spite in her tone. "But he will, eventually. I mean, think of everything I have to offer. And Caleb's engagement party is the perfect time, too. You know, New Year, new life. New wife."

Her giggle was like nails on a chalkboard to Maya's nerves.

"Too bad you're all alone," Lilah crooned. "Is that why you've avoided coming home all these years? Because you didn't want everyone to ask questions about the lack of a guy in your life? Your dad said you were single. Still. That's too bad. Maybe I can fix you up with someone when you get here?"

"I don't need—"

Before she could reject Lilah's offer, the other woman's mouth was off and running, listing the variety of losers she figured might condescend to a date.

"Then there's Marty Lankin. You remember him? Played tuba in the marching band. He moved back in with his mom last month after his gastric bypass and he's ready to start dating," Lilah continued.

Maya's knees wobbled. What could be worse? Going home to the emotional pain and stress of seeing the father who'd betrayed her? Or touring the dregs of the Black Oak dating pool to affirm Lilah's assurance that Maya was a loser?

No way in hell she was going back.

Maya's heart sank as she shoved her hand through her hair.

This was her father, though. He might have let her down, he might have disappointed her. He was a criminal, a con and now apparently a lech. But that didn't mean he deserved the likes of Lilah Gomez.

"I've got to go," she muttered, disconnecting over the other woman's protests.

Maya didn't know how long she stood there with her fist

clenched around the now-dead phone. The jungle of plants was a big green blur and her mind was filled with the sound of her own harsh breathing.

Finally, with a quick shake of her head and a couple of deep breaths, she forced herself to saunter back into the restaurant, putting a little extra swing into her hips as she did. Dave's gaze locked on her like a missile on a target.

See. She didn't need to be fixed up with momma's boy losers who lived in their parents' basements. Grateful to Dave for saving her ego, she gave him an extra-warm smile.

He responded with a loud gulp.

"Maybe we can do something special after the party this weekend," he suggested.

"This weekend?"

"It's my company's Christmas party," he reminded her. "I've got to go. Big promotion in the works, appearances count and all that. You're still going with me, right?"

A loud, raucous party filled with people she didn't know? Or preparing to go home and face her past, with all its nasty little demons and emotional pitfalls.

"Of course I'm going with you," she gushed. "There's nothing I'd rather do."

SIMON DIDN'T KNOW EXACTLY what Maya's intentions were, but she was definitely a woman on a mission. From what he'd overheard at lunch the previous week, Tobias was up to something new. Something she wasn't happy about.

He wondered if that had anything to do with the news he'd gotten two days ago. An ATF connection of his had let it slip that there were a slew of stolen guns spreading through Northern California. The Bureau of Alcohol, Tobacco and Firearms had narrowed the epicenter of the leak to the Santa Cruz Mountains. Which just happened to be where Tobias Black was. Coincidence? No way in hell.

This was Simon's shot. If he could bust Tobias Black, his career would skip the fast track and hit rocket speed. All he had to do was make a solid contact with the old guy's daughter. She was his entrée. A couple more conversations with her and he'd be able to claim her a friend when he visited Black Oak.

As if proving she was ready to be his new best friend, Maya chose that moment to stroll in, her arm tucked into the elbow of her guy friend. Despite the party in progress, Simon could clearly see the tension in the set of her shoulders, and the way she kept her body from curving into pretty boy's.

It shouldn't be too hard for Simon to move himself in. A little charm, a little distraction and a little luck were all he needed to pull this off.

He timed it carefully, putting himself in Maya's line of sight, careful to look like a guest by exchanging friendly chit-chat with strangers. Out of the corner of his eye, he caught her frown, satisfied when it turned to heated curiosity.

He had to wait about an hour before pretty boy left to head to the bar and refill their drinks.

Then Simon made his move. He strode over to where she stood silhouetted against the wide bank of windows.

"Hello," he said. "We've met, haven't we?"

It was a lame line, but he was interested in seeing what she'd do with it. Gold eyes considered him for a second, then she nodded. "You were at the Braverment party last week, weren't you? I'm Maya."

"Simon Harris," he introduced himself, using one of his covers. Then to put her at ease, he spent the next five minutes making idle chitchat.

Mid talk about the party and the potential for investors, they heard a soft chime over the music.

"Excuse me," she said with an apologetic smile. Pulling her phone from her tiny purse, she glanced at the screen. The blood drained from her face, making her look like a wax doll in a horror movie.

"Are you okay?" Simon asked, quickly moving to her side. He glanced at the screen and winced. Having seen plenty of pictures of Tobias Black, he easily recognized the man in the photo. The brunette plastered over his chest like a wet T-shirt was new to him, but Simon figured no daughter wanted to see her father being used as a stripper pole.

A text flashed across the screen next.

Aren't we a cute couple?

Well, now, that was interesting. Simon watched as red heat washed over Maya's previously ashy complexion. Fury? The pictured coupledom clearly didn't sit well with her.

"Friend of yours?" he asked, knowing it was a risk to get so personal. But he figured she was pissed enough to ignore the impropriety in her need to vent.

Maya shifted her glare from the phone to his face. She shook her head like she was trying to toss off the anger. "An idiot determined to ruin his life, is more like it."

Perfect opening.

"That is a shame," he said, leaning in just a little more. Not for the job this time. But because he liked feeling the warmth of her, seeing her golden eyes dilate so they were almost all black, and hearing her breath catch in such a sexy little way. Nice to know he could pull her out of her anger.

Then, as if knowing Maya's attention had shifted, her phone chimed again.

They both looked down.

Simon frowned. What the hell? It was a picture of a wedding dress.

"Oh, hell no," she hissed. Muttering cursewords under her breath, her fingers flew over the tiny keyboard at the speed of light.

He watched the text fly into the ether, excitement stirring in his gut.

"So you're going home this weekend?" he asked, his tone as innocent as he could make it. "Where's home?"

Maya wasn't paying him any attention, though. Her gaze flew over the crowd until she gave a little hum. Then she absently patted Simon's arm and said, "Excuse me."

Shit. Just like that, she was gone. She didn't even bother with a backward glance. Simon's ego screamed almost as loud a protest as his body at the loss of her floral-scented warmth.

Dammit. He wasn't finished yet. He needed to make a stronger contact. To get some information that he could drop into casual conversation that'd lead her father to believe that the two of them were really friends. He watched her stride away, trying to decide if that had been a good contact or a wasted one. *Your daughter hated the girly accessory you were wearing in that photo* wasn't much of a topic starter.

DESPERATE FURY PROPELLED Maya across the dance floor and through the throngs of people surrounding the bar. Anger and worry duked it out in her belly as she thought of that picture. Tobias was a brilliant man, except when it came to women.

She couldn't stand it. No way she could let her father suffer a lifetime, or even another month, with the likes of Lilah Gomez.

"Dave?" She offered her date a bright smile that was only a little shaky with nerves, and tilted her head toward the patio. "Do you have a second?"

Frowning at either the nerves in her tone or the fact that she'd interrupted his golf story, he gave his work buddies a be-right-back gesture. Taking her hand, he led her into the relative quiet of the atrium. "What's up? You look a little tense."

Maya almost winced. *Oops.* Tense wasn't the kind of thing that made a guy want to run off for a wild weekend of family stress. She forced herself to smile, bright and cheery like she wasn't ready to scream. Or cry.

Remembering her father's basic rule of the con, distraction, she ran her hand up and down Dave's arm in a gentle caress. He leaned into her body as if ready to let her take those strokes in any number of other directions.

"I just found out I have to take a trip," she told him.

"Now?"

"No, for New Year's," she explained. Sliding her fingers down his arm, she trailed them over the back of his hand to play with his fingers. His eyes blurred satisfyingly. "I was hoping you'd want to go with me. You were saying you wanted to spend more time together. I thought this might be a fun way."

"The two of us? Go away together?" His grin was huge as he pulled her into his arms and gazed down at her face like he'd just snagged a fab Christmas present. "I'm in. Just say when and where."

"I'd planned to leave the day after Christmas," she explained. She let herself relax into his body as if confirming his assumptions of just what kind of entertainment that trip would include. But fairness demanded she share, "I'm going back to my hometown. My brother just got engaged and is having a big party for New Year's. I haven't been back in years, and everyone is going to be really excited to meet my boyfriend."

She lost him a little more with each word she spoke. His arms stiffened and he slowly leaned away from her body. Clearly that translated to horror and damnation in guy-talk. It was like watching the fog roll over the Golden Gate.

This, she realized, was yet more proof as to why she'd sucked as a con artist. She could have just led him on. Let him think they were off for some kinky sex fun and then used that lure to keep him at arms' length during the trip. But no, she had to be all honest and crap. She felt like smacking herself in the forehead.

"Look. Maya. Um…" He looked around desperately, as if hoping someone would come and rescue him. Then he grimaced and told her. "I like you. I'd like to go to bed with you. But that's it. Nothing personal, but I'm not a meet-the-family kind of guy."

"But—"

"Look, I've got to get back inside." Clearly torn between running away in a commitment-phobic hurry and being a polite date, his gaze bounced between the door with its freedom, and her face. "Can you… Um… I need to go."

She debated trying to save the situation, but realized it was pointless. She couldn't lie. She didn't feel strongly enough about him to take things to the next level. Not even to save her father.

"I'll see myself home," Maya said, her words as heavy as her shoulders. "Don't worry about it."

"It's not you," he claimed.

Before he could pitch the worn-out spiel, she waved him away. If she hadn't been so upset already, the speed at which he gratefully scurried off would have done serious damage to her ego.

This sucked. Swearing she could feel the wind from Dave's speedy retreat, she paced the cement walkway of the atrium. With its impeccable timing, her phone chose that second to chime. Like a reluctant witness to a train wreck, she forced herself to look at this round of horrible text news.

I told everyone you're coming. We're all so excited to see you. I've even got a date for you on your first night home. We'll double.

"Just shoot me, it'd be less painful," she muttered.

"But such a waste."

Shocked, Maya jumped and gave a tiny scream. She spun around, one hand trying to keep her heart from pounding out of her chest, and glared.

Simon Harris. The Southern-fried sex muffin.

"Where'd you come from?" she asked, desperately hoping he hadn't overhead Dave's rejection.

"I saw your friend inside," he told her, tilting his head toward the bar where Dave was back, chatting with his friends. "You seemed upset earlier, so I figured I'd check on you. Make sure you're okay."

He was so sweet. Maya sniffed, trying to contain the emotional overload of the night.

"So how about I cheer you up?" he said in that jovial tone guys used to try and get past emotional scenes. "What are your holiday plans? A big family get-together, I'll bet?"

That was the wrong thing to say, though. His words were the last straw. Tears gushed, frustration tangling with a sudden burst of homesickness.

Looked like the night actually could get worse.

3

OH, HELL. SIMON CRINGED.

He'd thought this was turning into a killer opening, but he wasn't sure he could handle waterworks like Maya's. Not even for a major bust.

"Going home sucks," she told him, sniffling back her tears. "My family and I, we had a big falling out a few years ago. I know there's probably no point being upset about not going. But a part of me was hoping this visit would mend fences and bring us all back together."

"Prodigal daughter?" Simon mused. He hadn't realized the estrangement between her and her father was that deep. Knowing how rotten his own parent issues made him feel, he took her hands and gave them a sympathetic squeeze. "That can't be a comfortable reunion."

"Not even close. And now I'm getting daily texts with all kinds of drama over me being single. Lots of manipulation and game playing," she told him, anger sliding through the hurt in her tone. "The only way to avoid it is to bring a boyfriend home with me. Otherwise I'm going to spend the week dodging ugly matchmaking attempts, uncomfortable family drama and a nasty old school friend determined to make this a miserable visit."

"Look, it sounds to me like you don't have a choice," he said. He was a federal officer. He shouldn't be swayed by a sob story, right? He wanted an in to Tobias Black and this was his chance, served up on a golden platter by the sexiest woman he'd ever met.

Do the job, he reminded himself.

"You need to face this stuff. Take it from me, avoiding family drama only makes it all worse." At least, he assumed it did. Given that he and his family had said their ugly good-byes years ago, he didn't know that time or avoidance could make his problems any worse.

"You're right," she murmured. She shoved one hand through her hair, the luxurious curls waterfalling over her shoulders. She gave him a considering look. There was a calculation in her eyes that made him wonder if he'd underestimated her. Her head tilted to one side, she pursed her lips and seemed to be thinking something through. Since he figured whatever it was could only benefit him, he offered her his nicest, encouraging-but-unthreatening look.

"But I can't go alone. Not if I have to face Lilah," she murmured.

Simon wracked his brain, but couldn't recall seeing anyone named Lilah in the list of Black family members. So who was she and why did she put that tight look on Maya's face.

Maybe the nasty texter?

Before he could ask, Maya shifted. She pulled back her shoulders, lifted her chin and gave him a look that made him just a little nervous.

"You said you're looking for investors, right? It's a big deal that you're putting together?"

Where was she going with this? Nothing to do but play along, Simon realized.

"Yeah, I've been trying for weeks now and if I don't get this deal nailed down before Christmas, it'll fall apart." He played it up, shoving his hand through his hair and acting frustrated. "There is so much riding on this, and I've had a lot of interest. But so far nobody's willing to commit."

She gave a little hum through lips pressed tight together, then as if she were forcing out the words before she could change her mind, she said, "What if I had money to offer? Not a lot, maybe ten thousand?"

"You're interested in investing in the app platform startup?"

"I'm interested in making a deal," she clarified.

This should be interesting.

"Um, in exchange for investing, and for using my contacts at Braverment to find other investors, I'd want something in return." She nibbled temptingly on her bottom lip.

"Like what?" And where the hell was he going to find an app startup to invest in?

"In exchange, you go home with me and pretend to be my boyfriend."

Holy shit. Maybe Santa Claus really did exist.

"Let me get this straight," he said. "You're willing to invest ten thousand in the startup I'm funding? And to put in word among the investors you work with that it's a great deal. And in exchange, all I have to do is spend a week with the prettiest girl I've ever seen?"

And make the bust of his career, cementing his upward climb to success?

"That sounds crazy, doesn't it?"

"Not at all," he returned, trying not to sound too enthusiastic. "It sounds smart to me."

"Right." She laughed, pacing the length of the patio again. "No, it does. You need to be able to focus on dealing with the family drama without worrying about entertaining, or fending off, a date. But you need a boyfriend to avoid the matchmaking drama and give you a sort of touchstone to your current life. You know, so you don't get pulled too deep into the emotional stuff."

Her eyes wide and glistening with tears, Maya stopped mid-pace to nod slowly. "You're right. But that's all for my good. But you don't seem like you're doing so bad at finding investors that you'd have to resort to this kind of thing."

"Times are tough," he told her. "The economy sucks, computer startups are all over the place. If I didn't personally know the guy heading this up and know he's brilliant, I'd probably walk away myself. But I promised him, and his mother, that I'd make sure he had the resources to give his dream a shot. So you're saving my ass."

Simon wondered if he'd gone too far over the top. But that seemed to be just the right tone, since the skepticism faded from Maya's eyes. Instead she looked like she was seriously considering the deal.

Triumph was so close, Simon could taste it.

But…

His gaze traveled down over her body, noting that she once again wore a dress that covered her from neck to mid-thigh, yet screamed hot and sexy. The way the midnight blue fabric draped and hugged her curves made his fingers itch to see if the fabric was soft enough to touch that glorious flesh.

No. Even though his hardening body screamed in protest, he put on the mental brakes. That wasn't a road he was going down. She was a case. A tool at the most. Sexy, gorgeous and apparently fun, but still a means to an end.

She was so damned hard to resist. Telling himself it was all in the name of the job, he took her hands again, lifting them both to his mouth. He brushed soft kisses over her silky knuckles, then placed her hands, palms flat, against his shoulders.

"I need to get this out of the way," he said quietly. "It's got nothing to do with the deal, and everything to do with how I'm feeling."

She shook her head, looking like she wanted to protest. But instead her fingers dug into his shoulders.

Thighs brushing a tempting invitation against hers, his hands smoothed down the tiny curve of her waist to the sweet roundness of her hips. Her breath shuddered, just a little. Simon almost groaned aloud. She was so delicious. Was the reality of her as tasty as the promise?

Totally forgetting his plan—hell, his own name—Simon pulled her closer, so their bodies were close. So close, but not quite touching. Her warm scent wrapped around him like its own caress, making his mouth water, his dick harden.

Crazy, he thought, as he leaned down to take her mouth with his.

Their lips brushed, soft and sweet. Just this side of innocent. Safe, he told himself. A Happy Holidays kind of kiss. Totally acceptable.

Then she made this tiny sound. Somewhere between a purr and a growl, deep in her throat.

And he lost it.

His mouth took hers. His tongue slipped between her full lips, taking hers in a dance as old as time. He coaxed, he battled, he challenged. And damned if she didn't do exactly the same.

Simon's body screamed in pleasure. Passion, way out of line for such a simple kiss, demanded release. His muscles tensed as he forced himself to not grab her and find a dark corner to explore just how good this could get.

Having to grab control before he went over the edge, he pulled his mouth from hers. Her eyes were closed, thick dark lashes curving over the tops of her cheeks. She took a deep breath and slowly lifted those lashes.

Absolutely crazy. Breathless, Simon stared into her deep,

golden eyes and wondered if she was the answer to his prayers. Or the curse that would finally take him down.

Her hands were trembling and there was a sheen of shocked worry in her pretty gold eyes. Like she'd been just as overcome by that as he had. Before, he'd have taken her as a woman used to using her body to get what she wanted. He'd have been wrong.

"This wasn't what I offered to pay you for," she protested breathlessly. "I was offering to pay you cash. To help you with your investments. I don't barter with anything else."

Simon had no idea why it thrilled him that she'd never pulled a con using the oldest lure in the book. That made their kiss, well, special. And that, he winced, made him a sap. A horny, deceiving sap.

But still, he couldn't lie to her.

"Look," he said, risking the case by reaching out to take her hand, "I'm not going to deny I think you're a gorgeous woman. You're fun and I'm very attracted to you."

Her fingers stiffened and she tried to pull away. But Simon didn't let go.

"But I'm not the kind of guy who takes advantage of women." At least, not in the way she was worried about. "This deal is for me going home with you for New Years. I provide distraction and run interference with your family and that woman who keeps bugging you. That's all you're paying me for."

Her fingers relaxed and she gave a shaky sigh.

Then, because he couldn't help it, Simon added, "Anything else that happens? That's between us. Just you and just me. No deal, no investment, no family stuff. Just attraction."

He saw her throat move as she swallowed nervously.

"I know it was my idea, but I have to think it through. This is my family we're facing. I have to be sure it's not a mistake," she said. "If you give me your number, I'll call you in the morning."

Then, as if she were scared of what else might come out of her mouth, she gave him a quick smile, turned on those sexy heels and hurried back into the ballroom.

Simon watched, mesmerized by the sweet sway of Maya's hips as she waltzed away. All curves and sweeping dark curls, she was pure female. Pure delight. Pure temptation.

And she was going to be difficult to resist. But if Simon prided himself on anything, it was on his control. Which, he realized with a sigh and shake of his head as she shot him a look over her shoulder before leaving, was going to be sorely tested.

At least, it would be if she took him up on his offer. And he was pretty sure she would. She needed to go home, and was desperate to do so on her terms. The loss of pretty boy put her at a disadvantage.

Simon grinned. Things were working out even better than he'd hoped.

Before he could really dig into the joy of gloating, his cell phone rang. He glanced at the display and frowned.

"Don't you need probable cause to spy on me?" he answered.

"No clue what you're talking about," Hunter shot back, sounding amused. "I'm just checking in, seeing if you're ready to report to work tomorrow."

"Tomorrow is Sunday."

"Technically, today is Sunday. Which makes tomorrow the day you are due to report to the Savannah office for your next assignment."

Hunter must be on the east coast since it was only ten here. Still, Simon glanced around the atrium, narrowing his eyes at the windows and dark corners.

"About that…"

"Yes?"

There was no inflection in Hunter's voice, but still, Simon had the feeling that the man knew exactly what he was about to say. And wasn't happy about it.

"I've caught an opening on a cold case. I'm going to touch base with Roberts about pursuing it for the next week instead of taking a new assignment," he said, referring to his director.

"No."

"No?" Frowning, Simon strode to the back of the atrium, squinting at plants and barrels as he went. Did Hunter have that authority?

"As of now, you're temporarily assigned to my division. Your permanent move to the task force will depend on your work over the next month."

Stopping midstride, Simon struggled to decide how he felt about that. He'd worked damned hard for that transfer to Savannah. It was the next step up the ladder and he'd worked his ass off for it. But working with Hunter? That'd make his career.

All he'd have to do was give up his shot at Tobias Black. The shot he'd just cemented.

Maybe he should fill Hunter in. He instantly decided against it, though. He wanted to make this bust himself. He wanted to prove he deserved the promotion he'd just been offered.

Why *had* he just been offered that promotion?

"I didn't put in for a transfer. What's the deal?" he asked.

"I have need of your talents."

Simon was good. Damned good. But he had no illusions. Other than the fact that he had a photographic memory for numbers, there was nothing he could do that dozens of other agents couldn't. Not as well, but that was beside the point.

"Why do I doubt you?"

"Because you're an untrusting soul, Barton."

True. Simon sighed, his mind racing as he stepped out the back door to the hotel's deck. He glanced around, noted the stairs leading to the exit and headed that way. "I have personal time coming. I need to take it. I'll report to you in the DC office a week from tomorrow."

"Are you going to tell me what you're up to?"

Making his way down the series of stairs to the parking garage, Simon thought of Hunter's warning to step off the Black case. "Nope."

Hunter's sigh was silent. But Simon knew it was there. He grinned, pulling his keys from his pocket.

"I'll be in touch."

Simon's grin dimmed a little. In touch could mean so many things. In Hunter's case, it'd probably mean Simon would wake up tomorrow morning to the guy staring at him from the foot of his bed. But before he could protest, his new boss hung up.

Well, shit.

Sure, he had the perfect inside track to Tobias Black. A chance to guarantee his permanent position on Hunter's team and send his career skyrocketing. And now, it seemed like Hunter didn't trust him.

Crazy.

Except, Simon sighed as he slid into his car, he hadn't proved very trustworthy tonight. Gaining entrée to a criminal circle was one thing. But locking lips with that entrée was bad form.

Still, he couldn't regret that kiss.

Maya Black was delicious. Sweet. Freaking out-of-this-world amazing.

No matter how the rest of the case turned out, tonight was going down as a winner in his book.

THIS WAS A CRAZY PLAN. She should cancel. Maya's fist clenched around the phone she'd taken to carrying around the house in preparation for calling Simon. She should cancel. That was the only smart thing to do.

Cancel their deal. Call Caleb with the excuse that she was sick and couldn't make it. That'd give her time to figure out what to do next.

But if she waited, Lilah would have time to get a tighter hold on Dad. She'd sucker him into a wedding before Valentine's. As hurt and disappointed as Maya was in her father, she didn't think she could live with herself if she didn't do whatever she could to save him from that.

So she had to go through with it.

She'd bring Simon home. She'd pretend he was her boyfriend.

And she'd keep her fingers, lips and tongue off him.

The memory of her body pressed against his sent a wave of desire pounding through her. Her heart raced, heat surging, damp and needy, between her thighs. Yeah, that last one would be the hardest.

She looked around her lovely little haven of a house and sighed, her heart heavy. Yes, she'd be coming back. But things wouldn't be the same. No matter what happened in the next few days, she'd return a changed person.

A knock at the door prevented her from sinking too far into a pout strong enough to require chocolate fudge ice cream.

Maya hurried to the front, then, her hand on the doorknob, she stopped and took a deep breath. She wiped her suddenly damp palms down her jeans, tugged at the waist of her white angora sweater and fluffed her hair.

Pathetic, she chided herself with an eye roll. She was primping like a giddy virgin on her first date.

Squaring her shoulders, she grabbed the knob again and opened the door.

"Simon," she greeted, infusing as much airy confidence

as she could scrape together in her voice. "I'm not sure if I'm impressed or worried that you prepared so quickly for this little trip."

"Hey, you made an investment," he said, leaning against her door looking so hot and sexy she actually felt the need to fan herself. "All I had to do was throw some clothes in a bag when you did."

"No job worries?"

"It's easy to get time off during the holidays." He gave a dismissive shrug. "Not too many people looking to invest money this time of year. As the last week proved. But hey, this works out to both our advantage. Ya gotta love win-win deals, right?"

"Right." Maya shivered. There it was again. Something edgy under the amiable demeanor that had her both nervous and excited.

Forcing herself to stick with the plan, she stepped back and welcomed him in. Not that she was stupid enough to hope this wasn't a mistake. She knew it was. Her father had taught her at a young age to take the big risks but mitigate the damages.

"I'm all packed and ready to go," she said, waving a hand toward the modest stack of five suitcases, topped by a bright purple cat carrier. "You don't mind that I drive, right? I know the way and am more comfortable in my car. Besides, it's cold in the mountains and we'll likely hit bad weather and I'm betting my Ridgeline will handle it better than whatever sporty trick you drive."

"You keep a car in the city?" he asked, giving her a speculative look. But he didn't deny that he drove a sporty trick, she noticed.

"Public transportation is all well and good, but I prefer being in control."

He quirked a brow, but didn't comment. Instead he pulled his phone out of his pocket.

"Problem?" she asked.

"I'm less about control and more about convenience, so I rented a car for the trip. I'm calling the rental company to pick it up."

Lips pursed, Maya watched him make his call. That was the first lie she was sure he'd told her. This was not a man who ever chose convenience over control unless he already had all the cards stacked in his favor.

She shrugged into a light denim jacket while he finished his call. Then Simon approached her baggage.

"You're bringing a cat?" Simon asked, frowning at the carrier like it might hold some kind of explosive device.

"Of course. You don't think I'd leave her here, do you?"

"I can't say I thought about it at all, as I didn't know you had a cat. But is it a good idea to lock an animal in a cage for a couple hours? Won't it protest?"

"*It's* name is Dottie, and she's a good traveler," Maya said, walking over to lay her hand on the carrier. She rubbed the furry little face staring at her. Unconditional love purred back, soothing Maya's worries for just a second. "She won't be any problem."

He looked around her living room in a way that made Maya feel like he was trying to memorize the space. "You have a roommate, don't you?"

Maya gave him a sweet smile, tucked one long curl behind her ear and tilted her head to the side. Brow arched, she patted the carrier and said, "Dottie goes."

Then she waited. Would he pull out a fake allergy, a bossy attitude or cave like a wimp?

"I guess it'd be quite ungentlemanly to separate a lady and her kitty cat," he said with a shrug before pending over to peer into the carrier, then ribbing Dottie's nose through the bars.

Her smile dimmed.

How was she going to deal with him when he didn't follow any prescribed moves?

Simon straightened and gave her a wicked sort of grin. Before Maya could decipher it, he stepped forward and trapped her against the wall.

He smelled so good. Manly, with just a hint of soap. A smile played around his mouth but his eyes were intent and dark with desire.

"What are you doing?" she asked, horrified that her words sounded so breathless. But it was hard to help that, since she had no air in her poor, passion-shocked lungs.

"I figure we need a little practice," he said, his hands curving tighter over her hips and pulling her close. Not quite close enough to feel the sexy planes of his hard body against her softer one. But enough to warm her with sparks of desire, heating their way through her system like a burgeoning wildfire.

"Practice?"

"You don't want to look like we've never done this before, do you? If we're going to pull off the boyfriend-girlfriend thing, we should look comfortable together."

"Right," she said, not caring what he'd just said. Her eyes were locked on his lips, craving to taste again the full curve of that lower lip, to delve into the delicious heat of his mouth. He could make up all the bullshit excuses he wanted. She just wanted him to hurry up and kiss her.

Like he'd read her mind, he lowered his mouth to hers. Lips, soft and gentle, sipped and danced. He tasted so good. Rich. Strong. Decadently tempting. Desire moved like wildfire, zinging through Maya's body at a pace way too fast for the tempo of this kiss.

Maya wanted more. She wanted intensity, passion, the wild dance of a screaming orgasm. The dance she knew Simon could take her on.

Before she could dig her fingers into his hair and take them on the first step of that dance, Simon brushed her lips one more time, then slowly pulled back.

His eyes, almost black with desire, stared for a second. Then he blinked and shook his head.

"Grab the cat and let's hit the road," he said.

Maya allowed herself a second to lean against the wall until her knees didn't feel like jelly, then sucked in a deep breath and grabbed her purse and two bags.

This was going to be a very interesting trip.

4

IT'D BEEN MORE THAN two hours since he'd tasted Maya, and Simon was still way too uncomfortably hard to be stuck in a damned car. Even one as comfortable as her Ridgeline. He glared at the icy road, wishing for a brief second he were out in the freezing rain for just a few seconds.

"Car sick?" Maya said, not taking her eyes off the winding road.

"No. Why do you ask?"

"You keep looking out the window like you'd rather run alongside than stay in your seat."

"Maybe I'm not used to someone else in the driver's seat," he said, turning in his seat to watch her. She'd pulled her hair back into a tail that curled riotously down the shoulder of her denim jacket.

"Are you one of those guys who always has to be on top?" Maya teased.

Simon grinned, not only at the inference, but because as soon as the words were out, she winced like she wanted to grab them back. He figured flirting was probably second nature to her. From what he'd seen, though, it was something she tried, hard, to repress. He wondered why.

And he wondered how hard it would be to tap into that

nature and keep her flirting. And to see where things could go from there.

"You do a great job behind the wheel," he shot back, reaching out to trail one finger down the back of her hand. Because he was watching so closely, he saw her pulse jump in her throat. But her hands stayed steady on the wheel. "I'm betting you're just as good on top. You ever want to prove it to me, just say the word."

Her knuckles paled on the wheel and he heard her breath hiss, but she still didn't take her eyes off the road. His brows rose and his grin widened. She was amazingly controlled.

And he wanted, so badly, to break that control. What would it take? Could he do it with his mouth alone? Before she was undressed? He'd bet he could.

He wasn't sure she'd take that bet, though.

And he shouldn't, either. Out of line, he warned himself. She was a part of his investigation. He'd spent the night thinking about Hunter's call and the transfer. He had a shot at shaving five years off his climb up the ladder with that transfer. He'd be so much closer to Deputy Director. All he had to do was make the transfer permanent. And nailing the Black case would do that for him.

Which didn't mean he should nail Black's daughter in the process.

"So tell me about the town. Black Oak, right? Did you grow up here?"

Slowing to take a turn, she shot him a quick glance. In her molten-gold eyes he saw both curiosity and irritation. And there, just beneath those emotions, was the flickering heat of desire.

Crap.

Given the three, he'd take the curiosity. He never liked irritating a lovely lady, and he didn't think he could resist her desire. But he'd spent his life faking out people's curiosity.

"Black Oak?" he prompted. "Home sweet home?"

"It's a quaint little town at the foot of the Santa Cruz Mountains," she said slowly, obviously trying to figure out which of his mixed signals to respond to. "They get a fair amount of tourism, which downtown plays to nine months out of the year. We're visiting during the off-season."

"Does the town depend on tourism?" He could write for the local chamber of commerce, he knew so much about Black Oak. But he didn't know it from Maya's perspective.

"Somewhat. There are a lot of hikers and backpackers, tour groups and weddings that keep things interesting. About half the town focuses on that, the other half commutes to outside jobs."

Which jibed with his own information.

"And your family? Have they lived there long or are you a California transplant?"

"I was born in Black Oak," she said with a jerky shrug of one shoulder. "Grew up there until I left for college."

"And you still have family there, right? Am I about to meet a big family or small?" He kept his words light, friendly and conversational. Like he wasn't really curious but just making small talk.

She took a breath. For the first time since he'd kissed her, she looked a little shaky. Her fingers flexed on the wheel and she gave a tiny shrug.

"My father's family goes back to the founding fathers. They've always been pretty solid in Black Oak. Banking and law, for the most part. On the Parker side—that's my mom's family—my aunt is Her Honor, the Mayor."

"Friends in high places, huh?"

"More like overprotective babysitters," Maya said, her smile flashing. "There's no such thing as tolerating teenage high jinks in the Parker family."

"Did you generate a lot of teenage high jinks needing toleration?" He could imagine her as a teen. Same long black hair. Same huge gold eyes. Fewer curves, less overt sex appeal, but he'd bet she knew how to wrap those high school football players around her tiny finger. "Cheerleading escapades? Pep rallies run amuck? A half hour past curfew a few times too many?"

Her smirk was fast and wicked. And told Simon that while any and all of those scenarios might have played out from time to time, they were just the decorative sprinkles on top of a fluffy, frosted cupcake. The kind with a rich, decadent filling that you only found after you bit into it. Yeah, he'd bet that was Maya, even ten years ago.

"As I'm sure you'll hear during our visit, I was a model child. Angelic, even."

"Angelic?" Simon couldn't keep the doubt from his tone. Not even decorative sprinkles were angelic.

"Hey, I was adorable. Everyone loved me," she protested with a laugh. "My aunt always swore that my brothers sent her screaming for Lady Clairol. But I was her pride and joy. Well-behaved, smart and only sassy enough to keep me from being a pain in the ass."

"And was your aunt right?"

Slowing to turn into a long driveway flanked on either side by a white picket fence, she gave him an arch look. "What do you think?"

"I think your aunt had a soft spot for you and you never tried to ruin her opinion."

"And I think you're a smart man," she responded with a smile. "My aunt never wanted to see me as I really was. But it made her happy to think I was such a good girl. It also pissed off a lot of gossipy girls because they never found any real dirt on me, and it made my brothers, the brats, look even worse than they really were. All primary goals in my teenage heart."

"And your parents?" he asked, deeming it a natural question at this point in the discussion.

Her smile dropped away. Simon grimaced. Natural, but unwelcome.

"My mom died," she said quietly. She pressed her lips tight, sighed then shot him a look from the corner of her eye. "We lost her to cancer when I was one."

"I'm sorry," he murmured. And he was.

As they wound through the twisty two-lane highway, Simon stared out at the passing scenery. Tall trees, green hills, bucolic splendor. But he barely saw it.

His own mother had gladly shoved him out of the nest at seventeen. To make sure he didn't try to fly back, she'd moved without a forwarding address. Even after he'd had the resources, he hadn't bothered looking her up. He was happier going through life unencumbered. But he could hear the pain in Maya's voice. It must have hurt her terribly to grow up motherless.

He knew the facts from Tobias's file. He'd lost his wife to leukemia. He'd spent the next year in a fog of drunken despair. The aunt had tried to get custody of the kids, which had pulled him out of his fog. He'd rallied, gathered his kids close and for all appearances, become Mr. Mom for the next eighteen years.

Of course, the entire time he'd been running major cons. Some agents speculated that he'd run them both with and without his children over the years. But Maya was the only one who'd ever been caught.

Ready to steer the conversation in her father's direction, he leaned forward just a bit, to get a better view of her face.

"Here we are," she said before he could volley his first shot.

"What?" Startled, Simon looked around. "This isn't a town."

"No. This is the Black Oak Manor, just outside of town. I've reserved rooms here."

"Rooms?"

She flicked off the engine and turned in her seat, laying her arm across the steering wheel. The look on her face was pure feminine power, with just a hint of smoky interest. The kind that hinted at heat. Then she blinked and the look was gone, with only confused worry left in her intriguing eyes.

"You didn't think we were sharing a room, did you? I thought we'd covered that." She sounded hesitant, like she was worried he'd push the subject.

Answer that without looking like an ass, Barton. Despite those hot kisses, he really hadn't thought twice about their sleeping arrangements. She was his ticket to Tobias, not his ticket to a sex-fest.

"I guess I thought we'd be staying at your parents'…" He made a show of grimacing. "I mean, at your dad's. Or your brother's place or something."

He looked out the window and grimaced at the overabundance of nature everywhere. Trees and mountains, bushes and flowers, it was like the greedy fingers of nature were trying to gobble up the stately house. The house, in putting up a good fight, had a pillars and a spindled railing surrounding it, and what looked like thorny rose bushes at the windows and three stories of shuttered windows all brightly glinting back at the sun.

"How far from town is this?" he wondered.

"A couple of miles."

"I didn't realize Black Oak was that small," he muttered as he unhooked his seat belt.

"They have an inn downtown," she said, shifting her body so she could get her purse out of the back. Her shoulder brushed his arm, her flower scent filling his senses.

"Too close for comfort?" he guessed.

She shot him a look, both surprise and speculation in her eyes. "A little."

Simon nodded, hiding his grimace as he exited the vehicle. Two miles from town and Maya held the car keys. He waited while she gathered her kitty cat carrier, then followed the sweet sway of her denim clad hips up the cobblestone walk.

This case was continuing to be quite the challenge.

LATER THAT EVENING, Maya stood on the sidewalk outside the most opulent house in the town of Black Oak, watching the sparkling white lights as they flickered against the ice-chilled yard. Winter had hit hard in the Santa Cruz Mountains.

"Wow," Simon said quietly, stepping up next to her. He shook his head at the deep purple paint and gilded railing, then scanned the yard filled with lawn art and elaborately manicured bonsai bushes. "Is that a naked angel statue?"

Maya glanced at the six-foot tall marble depiction of— she squinted—*Eros?* "I think he's supposed to be the god of love. Caleb's future mother-in-law is, um, unique. I'm pretty sure that's Dionysus, the wine god over on the other side of the walk."

"Huh," he said, stuffing his gloveless hands in his pockets and rocking back on the heels of his cowboy boots. He continued to look around, clearly fascinated.

"Caleb said Pandora thought her mom's house would be the best place for us all to meet for dinner. Neutral territory, if you will."

That'd been Maya's first inkling that she was going to like her new sister-in-law.

"Do you think there are more naked statues, of the female sort, inside?" Simon mused.

"I don't remember her old house being quite this entertaining," she mused. "She must drive my aunt crazy."

"Your aunt?"

Maya gestured to the gray house with its carefully mani-cured lawn, tidy junipers and plain white-curtained windows closed tight as if horrified by the view.

"Her Honor, the Mayor lives next door to the town psy-chic," Maya explained. Despite her fleece-lined jacket and leather gloves, she shivered a little looking at her aunt's house. Oh, the lectures she'd endured there. Tea, cookies and decorum every Monday after school.

Still, Aunt Cynthia had loved her, in her way. And she'd kept the connection to Maya's mother alive through stories and pictures. Maya sighed softly. Disapproving lectures were a small price to pay for that little piece of her mom each week.

She glanced at Cassiopeia's driveway, noting the Harley, a classic Chevelle and a late model Honda.

"It looks like almost everyone's here," she mused. "Pan-dora, that's Caleb's fiancé, she said it'd just be family. Her and her mom, my brother and, um, our father. Again, the goal being less awkwardness."

She was stalling. She knew it, and a glance at Simon's sympathetic face said he knew it, too. But her stomach was doing somersaults and her insides were shaking. Her love life wasn't top of her priorities right now but she was pretty sure throwing up on Eros's feet would doom it forever.

"Wanna leave a note on the door and run away?" he teased.

At the same time, he reached out and took her hand. Her heart melted a little at the move. She knew she should pull away. Pretend she was strong and could handle this, no prob-lem. But his touch calmed some of the nerves. Made her feel safe at the same time as it made her feel special. And just a little excited. So instead, Maya sighed, then curled her fin-gers into his. This was going to suck, unquestionably. So she'd take any comfort she could get.

"Running away never works," she said with a sad smile. "At least, not for long."

She'd filled him in on the bare bones of the family dynamics, that she and her father were estranged and her brother had been traveling for his career for the past half-dozen years. But she'd skipped over the finer details, figuring nobody else was going to bring up her arrest record and her father's betrayal over dinner.

"Then shall we?" He gestured with their entwined hands toward the door. "If things get too stressful, we can sneak off for a makeout session."

That shocked a laugh out of Maya. She turned toward him, her stiletto boots hitting a patch of ice on the sidewalk. With his free hand, Simon grabbed her shoulder to steady her. Her breath a fog between them as she puffed out a relieved sigh at the near miss, Maya looked up to thank him.

And got lost in the green depths of Simon's eyes. They were mesmerizing. Gorgeous and hypnotic, she could stare for hours. There was something in the depths, something that made her feel safe. To want to trust him with all of her secret hopes and dreams.

He stepped closer, so their bodies brushed together. They were both wrapped in heavy winter coats. Hers fleece-lined denim, his a snow-worthy parka. But she swore, she could feel the heat of his body through the layers. It warmed her. It tempted her. It made her insides melt.

"Maybe this will take your mind off of being nervous," he said, sliding his hands under her hair to curve over the back of her neck. His fingers were chilly, a vivid contrast to the warmth of his body as he pulled her close.

"This is…"

His lips brushed over hers, making her swallow the word *crazy*. But she didn't stop thinking it.

Crazy wild.

His lips were so sweet. So soft as they rubbed over hers. His tongue slipped, so gently, along the edge of her lips. She gasped, opening her mouth to his. Taking that as a welcome, Simon's tongue moved in to dance with hers.

Crazy hot.

Their mouths sipped and slid. Hot and wet. She gasped when his teeth nipped at her lower lip. He soothed the tiny hurt with his tongue, then sucked her lip into his mouth. Desire took on a sharp edge. Maya's fingers dug into the thick cushion of Simon's parka.

Crazy intense.

His hands shifted, smoothing down the sides of her throat, along the edge of her collar. Warming her skin and leaving a sizzling trail of heat behind. Heat that made her want to strip off her jacket and bury his hands inside her blouse. To feel his fingers on her. To find out if they were as talented as his mouth promised.

Finally, just as she was wondering if her knees would hold up long enough for her to throw him in the back of her truck and strip him naked, he pulled away.

He stared down at her, his eyes dark with desire. His fingers tightened briefly on her shoulders before he slid them down her arms to take her hands in his.

"Well," Maya said breathlessly. But she couldn't think of anything to say after that. Her brain was blank, her body a puddle of churned-up lust. All she could do was blink and try and reinflate her lungs.

"Well," Simon echoed, his voice a little hoarse. But he seemed to have a few brain cells still working, because he looked around, then tucked his arm around Maya's shoulders. He took a deep breath. Then, pulling her along, he headed up the walk toward the front door.

"Wait," she protested halfway there, realizing they were heading for the lion's den and she wasn't prepared.

"Best to do it now, while we're in a good mood," he said, giving her a wicked wink. Then, to her horror, he reached out one finger and rang the doorbell.

Maya spent one glorious second entertaining the fantasy of turning heel and running away. But given that Simon had a good grip on her shoulders, she'd probably trip and land face first at Eros's naked feet.

Letting the image entertain, and sooth her, she took a deep breath. Before she could let it out, the door swung open.

"Well, hello," intoned the redheaded Amazon in a throaty voice. "You're Maya. And you—" she gave Simon a slow, appreciative once over "—are delicious. Please, join us."

The woman was wearing heels, making her easily six feet tall. Her dress was a midnight blue with tiny silver stars embroidered along the bodice and teeny gold planets along the hem. Crystal earrings as big as Maya's fist glinted in the porch light through an abundance of fire-engine-red waves of hair.

Wow.

"Cassiopeia, isn't it?" Maya asked as she stepped out from under Simon's arm to cross the threshold. "You did a great séance and tarot reading for my senior class event. I still remember how accurate and, well, a little scary, your words were."

Taking Maya's hand in her own, Cassiopeia offered a smile that was oddly reassuring. "Just, as I imagine, this evening feels to you now. But take heart, it'll all turn out just fine."

It wasn't so much her words that sent a chill through Maya. It was her tone of voice. Knowing, intense and just a little eerie.

Maya's smile stiffened and she pulled her hand free. Then both women looked back at Simon, who was still on the porch looking dumbfounded. At Maya's arch look, he cleared his throat and held out his own hand.

"Simon Harris, it's a pleasure," he said.

"I can't wait to learn all about you, Mr. Harris," Cassiopeia said, holding his hand in hers as she closed the door. Then she gave Maya a naughty wink, and led the two of them down a long magenta hallway.

"Darlings," Cassiopeia said as she entered the great room first. "Our guests have arrived."

Before Maya could get a look around, or even gauge how many people made up Cassiopeia's *darlings,* she was enfolded in a tight bear hug and swung off her feet in a wide, stomach-arching circle.

All thoughts, and thankfully her nerves, at looking for her father disappeared.

"Caleb," she squealed, her face buried in a hard shoulder. He smelled the same. Like Irish Spring soap, coffee and, well, like her big brother. His arms were tight around her waist as he set her to her feet and gave her a thorough inspection.

His eyes, the exact same shade of gold as her own, narrowed, like he saw something that worried him. Then he smiled, his teeth white against the dusky five-o'clock shadow he always seemed to sport.

"Hey, little girl."

"I missed you," she murmured, ashamed that her eyes filled with tears, but unable to stop them. "It's been so long."

"Too long. But that's done. Now you get to see me a minimum of three times a year, whether you like it or not."

"Three?"

He shrugged. "Arbitrary number. I'll take more, but refuse to settle for less."

"Bossy."

"Better believe it."

They grinned at each other. The old patterns, the teasing, the simple and easy affection. They were still there. A tiny part of Maya's heart, one she hadn't even realized she'd tucked away, sang in relief. Her entire body sagged with the joy of having her brother back in her world again.

"I want you to meet Pandora," Caleb said, stepping aside to take the hand of a slender, auburn-haired woman.

Maya stared. She'd had a solid idea of what kind of woman it'd take to bring down the mighty Caleb Black. Someone a little hard, a lot sexy, wild and in-your-face strong.

But while Pandora was sexy, and looked strong enough to handle Caleb, she was anything but hard. Instead, she looked…sweet, Maya decided. A soft fall of auburn hair brushed shoulders covered in a black velvet dress, hazel eyes looked back at Maya, both happy and just a little nervous.

"Maya, I'm happy to meet you. I remember you from school, but doubt you remember me," she said, stepping forward to offer her hand.

"That's my loss, then. And now I owe you," Maya said with a grin. "You not only snagged my brother, but you've got him to stay in one place. We're going to have a nice, long talk and you'll have to share all your secrets."

Pandora laughed, giving Caleb a look that told Maya that quite a few of her secrets would probably make his little sister wince.

"And look what Maya brought us," Cassiopeia said from the doorway, her arm still wrapped around Simon. Maya bit her lip at the look on his face. Baffled amusement combined with something curious. Edgy.

"Who's he?" Caleb snapped, slipping right back into overprotective big brother mode.

Her gaze shot to her brother, a frown creasing her brow. "Behave," she warned in a low voice.

Caleb's eyes met hers and for a second she thought he'd argue. She wondered if he gave criminals that look. But she had nothing to hide, nor did Simon. Well, except for faking their relationship and all. But that didn't count.

"Everyone, this is my boyfriend, Simon," she said, hurrying over to take Simon by the hand and rescue him.

"Boyfriend?" Caleb said, his gaze bouncing between the two of them. Maya scooched closer, pressing herself to Simon's side. Either not getting the hint, or not willing to use her as a most-likely-necessary shield, Simon didn't put his arm around her. Instead, the crazy man stepped away, then strode over to offer Caleb his hand.

"Simon Harris. Nice to finally meet Maya's family."

"It might be a short meeting if things don't chill out, fast," Maya muttered with a glare at her brother.

Caleb did take the hint, and accepted Simon's hand for a brief shake. Then he jerked his chin toward a bank of red, tufted velvet couches and said, "We'll talk."

"You will not," Maya said, shaking her head. "I'm here to meet your fiancée and hear all about the upcoming wedding. Not to have you bullying my friend. I mean it. Chill. Or we'll leave."

Instead of seeming worried by her big brother's posturing, Simon just stood between the two of them, a slight grin playing about his lips.

Maya narrowed her eyes in consideration. He obviously wasn't intimidated by Caleb. Her brow arched and her heart sped up just a little. She'd never, that she could remember, met anyone who wasn't intimidated by a Black man.

Her gaze skimmed Simon's calm, amused face and she sighed a little.

Nope. Never.

God, that was hot.

"Well, well."

All thoughts of heat, of amusement and even the joy of seeing Caleb again, they all fled at the sound of that voice.

Her mouth dried and her heart skipped a beat.

Simon must have read the stress on her face, because

amusement fled off of his, too. He went poker-faced, his shoulders tightening, his chin lifting just a bit. Like he was preparing for a battle.

She took odd comfort from that.

Stomach churning, she closed her eyes for a second to gather her composure.

Opening her eyes, Maya didn't know why, but she took Simon's hand. Neutral territory, maybe? Or so she could grab him and run out the door, probably.

Then, with a deep breath, she turned toward the hallway.

"If it isn't my little girl, all grown up," Tobias said, his grin as wide and infectious as always.

He looked older. And he looked exactly the same.

The thick, black hair he'd passed on to his children was graying a little at the temples, but his midnight-blue eyes were still bright and shrewd. He stood tall and strong, his hands shoved in the pockets of his khakis as he looked at her like a man starved for the view.

In those seconds, she remembered every wonderful thing about him. How he'd held her hand on the first day of school. Taught her to ride a bike, and mopped up her tears when Johnny Hanover had broken up with her in first grade. How he'd taught her to stand up for herself, to believe in herself, and to not be afraid to make things happen. How his eyes had filled as he'd watched her go on her first date. And how he'd always tugged on her curls and told her that she was the spitting image of her momma, the most beautiful woman in the world.

Her heart melted. Once a daddy's girl, always a daddy's girl, she couldn't stop the tremulous smile from curving her lips at the sight of him.

She took a single step forward, almost unconsciously. Then stopped like she'd been hit in the face by a brick wall.

"Hey, there, Maya," Lilah said as she sidled around Tobias, then like a disease, curled herself into his side. "I wasn't sure you'd show."

5

SIMON OBSERVED THE DRAMA play out. It was like watching an award-winning performance. One he'd missed the first act of, though. So now he was trying to fill in the blanks.

Not that it was difficult. The redheaded Amazon and her daughter were new to him, but their parts in this drama were pretty easy to figure out. Innocent distractions, with very little clue what kind of person Tobias was.

His eyes shifted to Maya's brother. About his own age, a few inches taller and a whole lot more menacing. The resemblance between Caleb and Maya was striking. Black hair and gold eyes, with those same intense cheekbones. Simon had researched Caleb Black before this weekend, and came up against a blank wall. The man existed, but his record was suspiciously whitewashed. Simon wasn't willing to tip his hand to Hunter by pulling any official strings. He'd figured he could rely on his own instincts. Instincts that were telling him that Maya's brother was nobody to mess with.

And then there was the family patriarch playing his role to the hilt. Simon had spent years studying Tobias Black's files. He'd seen plenty of photos, even video footage of the man. So he'd thought he was prepared. But there was a charisma about him that was surprising. Like his children, he was tall, with rich black hair that flowed back from a commanding face. His gaze was shrewd, his smile a warm invitation to open your heart, soul and wallet for his perusal.

Simon had to hand it to him, the man pulled off the air of a guy completely at ease, despite the fact that everyone in the room was glaring at him. Except the gal plastered against his side. She looked like the cat who'd gulped down a fish tank.

She was probably the one he should thank for his attendance at this little party. Clearly, there was some sort of competition between the two women.

It must be a girl thing. Despite her sultry air, Maya was pretty modest. The brunette, though, seemed a little more out there. Her clothes were tight, her hair was big and her smile flashed bright white as she wrapped herself around a man old enough to be her daddy.

Maybe he was biased, but Simon figured there was no contest in the looks department. But Lilah seemed nice enough.

"I'm so excited to see you again, Maya," she gushed, her words bubbling with sweetness. Heavily lined eyes swept the room, her smile bright and happy. "It's been, oh, just forever. And you brought a friend. Isn't that sweet. I'll tell you the truth, I've spent plenty of time worrying about you over the years. I mean, you have had some really bad luck at love, haven't you, Maya?"

Everyone in the room cringed, but the brunette kept rambling on about first loves and Maya's high-school boyfriend.

"Larry was this total jerk," Lilah told Simon. "The whole time he was dating Maya, he was seeing me, too. Behind each other's backs. Can you believe that?"

There seemed to be plenty more to that story if the looks on everyone's faces were anything to go by. Maya looked like she was going to scream. Caleb's teeth were set in a grimace and Tobias looked like he knew a bomb was about to explode, but wasn't sure how to diffuse it.

"Why don't we all take a seat," Cassiopeia interrupted, her tone soothingly hypnotic, like she was trying to calm a group of rabid animals, all of whom might attack at any second.

"Drinks?" Pandora, Caleb's fiancée, offered with a friendly smile that poured an aura of calm over the tense room. "And perhaps some canapés."

Cassiopeia hurried over to the sideboard to start the appetizer trays moving. But Simon didn't pay much attention.

All of his focus was directly on Maya.

She looked heartbroken.

His own chest ached a little as her defiant glare shifted between her supposed friend and her father. Betrayal was clear in every line of her body. Now was the time to man up and play his part. He'd promised her distraction and a buffer. With that in mind, he stepped closer and slipped his hand into Maya's.

After a brief spasm, like she might pull away, her fingers clenched his. She looked up at him with a grateful smile, which did nothing to hide the pain in her eyes.

"Let's sit," he suggested, keeping his words low and intimate. To jolt her out of the funk he could see her sliding into, he lifted their joined hands to his lips so he could brush a kiss over the inside of her wrist. Her breath caught. Like before on the front sidewalk, she seemed to forget her nerves in favor of a little love play.

Which clearly pissed off the men in her life. Too bad. At the moment he didn't care how it affected his case. Ignoring the twin glares coming at him from opposite ends of the room, Simon wrapped his arm around Maya's shoulder to lead her to a red velvet couch. They sat, close enough that her thigh was almost on top of his. As soon as he pulled his arm from around her shoulders, she gripped his hand again.

A surge of protective instincts rose to match the ever-growing, and slightly disconcerting, rising lust brought on by the feel of her warm body pressed against his.

The lust was totally inappropriate, especially considering the situation and other people in the room. But, dammit, her thigh felt so good against his. She was so close, he could smell the flowery spice of her perfume and the sweet apple of her shampoo.

Breathing deep, mentally breaking down an AK-47 to try and distract his body from embarrassing him, Simon leaned back into the couch cushion. He wasn't sure if he was pleased or just tormented when Maya followed, her body curving into his.

"So what's the deal?" Caleb snapped, his words shooting across the room with the speed and velocity of a bullet. "Where'd you two meet? How long have you been a...thing?"

"The length of my things are none of your business, big brother," Maya returned, offering him a saccharine smile. She sounded more amused than irritated, though. "I'd think you'd remember that, even after all these years."

Brow arched, Simon's gaze shifted from brother to sister. They were too busy grinning at each other to clarify the memory for the rest of the room, though.

"Caleb and Gabriel used to think big brother status gave them some say in Maya's dating life," Tobias offered, untangling himself from the brunette's clutches and coming into the room to take his own seat. "She let them get away with it when it served her purpose. Like getting rid of too-ardent admirers. But mostly she kept their noses out of her business."

"How do you keep Caleb out of anything?" Pandora wondered. True love or a bad case of hero worship, Simon wondered. Then she continued with a cute little laugh. "He's so bossy and pushy. I might need a few tips, Maya."

"A solid right hook, plenty of blackmail material and when necessary, a talent for sneaking down the trellis after dark,"

Maya told her future sister-in-law. Her tone was amused, her words easy and light. But her fingers still gripped Simon's like he was a lifeline.

"You were so mean to Caleb and Gabriel," Lilah said as she curled up on the arm of Tobias's chair. "Two of the sexiest boys at Black Oak High and you made their lives hell."

"Don't be silly, Lilah," Maya said, her words so sweet they dripped sugar. "It wasn't me that made their lives hell in high school. It was the girls who were always hanging out, pretending to be my friend so they could hit on my brothers."

"I have no idea what you're talking about," Lilah said stiffly. After a brief glare, she lifted her chin and shifted her attention to Tobias. "Sugar Bear, you should tell Maya our news."

There was enough tension in the room that Simon was surprised nobody grabbed a hold of it and beat the woman upside her smirking face.

"This is Pandora and Caleb's moment," Tobias said, giving the younger woman a swift, silencing look. "I think we should all toast the happy couple. And then, of course, we can get back to Caleb's earlier question."

Tobias waited a beat while everyone frowned in confusion, then he arched one dark brow and said, "Maya is going to tell us all about her relationship with this fine young man. A man that must be pretty amazing, given that she'd bring him home for her first visit in years."

The room's energy shifted yet again as all eyes focused on Maya and Simon.

"I think I'll skip the personal rundown," Maya said, her words tight. "I'd say we've done pretty well staying out of each other's lives for the last little while. Let's not ruin our record."

Simon had been in standoffs with vicious criminals that

had less intensity than the stare off between father and daughter.

Cassiopeia, the intrepid hostess, interrupted the paternal moment with a deceptively comfortable laugh. "So, this is going to be a mystery relationship. Won't it be fun to see what kind of tidbits we can get from you two this week?"

"Not so much a mystery as just private," Maya dismissed, her smile softening for the older woman. "And definitely not why I came home. Really, this week is all about Pandora and Caleb. Nothing else could have brought me home, just like nothing could keep me away from celebrating my big brother's happiness."

She pointedly shifted her body, angling it away from her father, resting her gaze on the happy couple. "So Pandora, did you come with endless patience and a big whip or will you be putting them on your wedding registry?"

Probably thrilled to stave off a potentially ugly confrontation, Pandora launched into the romantic story of her courtship.

Despite himself, Simon was drawn in by the tale. From the fact that her fingers no longer crushed his and because she relaxed enough to give the occasional giggle, he figured Maya was, too.

"And then I found out Caleb was actually here undercover, to bust a drug ring," she said, giving her fiancé an arch look. "A ring, I might add, that he thought I was a part of."

"Nope," Caleb interrupted, speaking for the first time since Pandora had started her history report. "Despite the intel, I always knew you were innocent. Or, I should say, not involved in a crime."

"Undercover?" Simon asked before he realized the word was out of his mouth. Stunned, he froze. He'd never broken cover. Never blurted out any thought, any words, that weren't sanctioned by the image he represented.

What the hell was wrong with him?

Then Maya shifted, her denim-clad leg sliding against his thigh in a way that made him desperately regret that they were in a roomful of suspects.

Aha. Maya was what was wrong with him.

"I guess it's okay to share now that it's over," she said after a quick glance to her brother for confirmation. "Caleb just retired from the DEA. He's temporarily taking over as Black Oak's sheriff until elections are held and he officially wins the position."

No wonder Simon had hit a blank wall when researching Maya's brother. His gaze shifted to Tobias. How'd that sit with dear ole dad? It looked like Maya wasn't the only Black kid to have father issues.

"Sounds exciting," he said, slipping back into character by infusing his words with just a hint of awe. "You must have some great stories to tell."

"What kind of stories do you have to tell?" Caleb asked with a chilly smile. "We still haven't heard much about you. What do you do, Simon?"

Simon hesitated for the space of a heartbeat, considering his options. If Caleb had government connections, he might have Simon checked out. If it were him, he would. But many others had tried, and none yet had broken his cover.

So...

"I'm an investment broker. I have a degree in macroeconomics, business management and speak three languages."

Only one of which was a lie.

Before Caleb could dive into his cross examination, there was a loud ring.

Tobias looked at the readout on his cell phone, pushed a button to silence it and slid the device back in his pocket. "I hate to miss out, but it seems there's a problem at the motorcycle shop that needs my attention. Besides, I'm sure Maya would like a little time to relax with Caleb without having to split her attention between that and her anger toward me."

"Oh, but I was hoping to spend time with Maya," Lilah pouted. "Or I could just wait here, get to know her friend. You can pick me up later? Or Simon can give me a ride home."

He debated for all of two seconds. Sure, the brunette would have info on Tobias and she was clearly the chatterbox type. But he could feel the angst emanating from Maya and figured she'd explode if he agreed.

"Nope, sorry. Maya and I were going to tour the town and see all her favorite hangouts after dinner," Simon lied with a bland smile. Smart casework, he told himself. It had nothing to do with wanting to protect Maya's feelings.

Still, he felt about ten feet tall when Maya sighed and gave his hand a warm squeeze.

"C'mon, Lilah," Tobias urged. The concerned look on his face told Simon that he, too, was aware of how stressful this was for his daughter. "The shop is only five minutes away but I've got to drop you first, so we need to get going."

Lilah didn't leave quietly. She tossed out a few more flirty innuendos and snarky comments on her way out. Then, finally, with an air-kiss for Maya and barely a word to the other women, she wrapped herself around Tobias and swayed out the door with her hips swinging like a pendulum.

Apparently not needing any more comfort, Maya released her death grip on Simon's hand and shifted so there was easily room for another person between them. Oh, she did it subtly enough, making a show of poking her brother in the shoulder and asking him how he liked being the law in town. But Simon got the message.

He'd served his purpose.

He tried to ignore how much he missed the warmth of her body against his.

"So, Simon, you're an investor?" Cassiopeia asked him as

she offered a tray of prosciutto-wrapped asparagus spears. She'd said they were special, so he took three. Tension made him hungry. "I'm surprised. I'd have guessed you did something dangerous or exciting. I'm sensing a lot of undercurrents and secrets in your aura."

"Leave his aura alone, mother," the sweet-faced Pandora chided. She gave Simon an amused look of apology. "She doesn't mean to poke and pry. She just can't help herself."

"Nothing wrong with a little curiosity," Simon said with a smile, biting into a tasty bit of asparagus. He watched Maya as she talked to her brother; words spilling out of her lush lips at about a mile a minute. Simon would love to be sitting closer, to hear what had her so animated and happy.

But the other women, obviously big on running interference for Caleb, kept his attention until Pandora announced it was dinnertime.

As he sat at the table with the secondary players, Simon analyzed the success of his evening. He'd made contact. His cover was holding and he was making inroads with the tight-knit Black clan. Not bad for his first night.

He glanced across the table at Maya. Animated and bubbly, she looked like she was having the time of her life. Until you looked closer.

He wished like hell that the pain in her eyes didn't rip at his gut. When had she started meaning so much to him? And how was she going to look at him later, when he'd arrested her father? Because feuding or not, she was still Daddy's little girl.

THIS WAS HARDER THAN she'd thought it would be. Maya stared out the passenger window as the glistening lights of the manor, bright and blurry through her tears, shone through the dark.

Until she'd faced her father, looked into the eyes of the

man who'd raised her, trained her, taught her everything she considered worth knowing, she'd thought it would be simple. Breeze into town, celebrate her brother's news while deciding if his fiancée was worthy of him. A maybe, dangle Simon in front of Lilah as a distraction, to lure her away from Tobias. Or better yet, "out" her for the tramp she was. Then, blithely ignore, for the most part, her father's existence.

Instead, she'd come away wondering how Caleb and Pandora had discovered the secret to true love. Then, rather than throwing Simon in Lilah's path, she'd glommed on to him like he was her own personal security blanket. And her father? She should have remembered that nobody, but nobody, ignored Tobias Black.

"Nice evening," Simon said. "Thanks for bringing me."

Blinking away the evidence of her little pity party, Maya shifted to look at Simon. She wasn't about to admit it to anyone, but she couldn't have gotten through tonight without him. He'd been a silent rock for her to hang on to, an amusing charmer distracting everyone when she'd needed a break.

And then there was that kiss.

"I'm glad you joined me," she said honestly. Then, giving in to a need that had been nagging at her, pulling at her concentration and playing out behind the scenes the entire night, she reached over and trailed her fingers in a light, teasing caress over his denim-clad thigh.

She gave a low hum, wondering if the hardness under her fingers was tension, or if he just had some deliciously muscled thighs. The urge to find out was overwhelming, filling her with an edgy kind of desperation. To feel more. To lose herself in discovering just what Simon had going on under those jeans.

"Wasn't Cassiopeia's reading interesting?" she said, keeping her words low as she shifted one knee toward the console so she could face him. And, delightfully, to give herself better petting access. Now her fingers were drifting up, along the deliciously rounded muscles of his biceps. "You know the one she did for the two of us. What did she call it? The Lovers' Outlook. Do you believe in that kind of thing? Intuition and such?"

He gave her a long look, like he was weighing her words and deciding exactly which direction he wanted to let the conversation head. That he thought he was in control here was clear.

Disabusing him of that mistaken belief was going to be a lot of fun.

"I was a little distracted by the cards she used," he said with a light laugh. "Those were some very well-endowed naked people on those pieces of paper."

"Measurement anxiety?" she teased, her fingers trailing down to his wrist and over the back of his hand where it lay on his thigh.

His easy smile slipped for just a second. Tension flashed through the car. Maya almost grinned, loving the power, the intensity of his reaction. If he was this easy to arouse with just a few words, a little challenge and a simple touch, what could happen later? When she really put some effort into it?

"No anxiety here, sweetheart. If you want, we can strip down and pose for that Lovers card. Bet we put those fancy sketches to shame."

"You think?" Maya asked. Then she slid the fingers of the hand that wasn't fondling Simon into her pocket and pulled out her cell phone. "I think my camera has a timer. We can test the theory."

"All we need is an oak tree that bears apples on one side," he mused. He made a show of looking into the dark forest beyond the B&B, then arched a brow. "Maybe we go looking tomorrow?"

"Tomorrow?"

"I'd imagine it's a little late to go tree searching," he reminded her, glancing at his watch. "Probably a little late to be huddled up in the car, too. Don't you think Dottie's getting lonely?"

The hard shell around Maya's emotions softened for the first time since she'd left home. Dottie always made her feel better. For the past four years, whenever she felt lonely or sad, she just cuddled up to the sweet black-and-white kitty. In a way, Dottie had become the unconditionally loving family Maya had missed when she'd left home.

And Simon was worried about her. How sweet was he? Maya sighed, her stress melting away.

Gone was her anxiety over how things would go seeing her dad again. The stress over facing the family and Lilah's nastiness faded. The nagging worry over what her father was up to, and she knew damned well he was up to something, relaxed.

Leaving behind awareness. All of the intense, thigh-melting sexual awareness that she'd been holding at bay all night. From the kiss they'd shared on the sidewalk to the gentle warmth of his hand in hers.

Speaking of hands, her gaze landed on his as he gripped the steering wheel. Large, rugged and competent. She ran her tongue over her lower lip, wondering again how good he was with those hands.

It was all she could do not to lean across the console and nibble on his fingers. Luckily they reached the manor before passion overcame sanity.

"We're here," he said with a smile.

She gave him a quick nod, waiting until he got out of the car before moaning with frustration. What was she supposed to do? She wanted to jump him, but after making such a big deal over this being purely business between them, she couldn't.

Could she?

Simon made it from the driver's side to her door before Maya had finished tucking her scarf in and zipping up her jacket. By the time she'd grabbed her purse from the back, he had the door open and his hand extended.

"Such the gentleman," Maya said, making sure her body slid against his when she exited. Sure, they had four or five layers between them, so the zings of passion that made her nipples rock hard and her panties a little damp were purely inspired by the hot attraction she had for him.

"A lady deserves the best," he said, shifting just an inch. Enough to trap her body between his and the car seat.

"And you are...?"

"Sweetheart, I'm the best at everything I do," he promised, his smile flashing in the moonlight.

"Fancy that. So am I."

"This should be interesting, then."

"Indeed," she agreed, reaching up to give his cheek a patting sort of caress. Then with a wink, she slipped around his body with as much physical contact as possible so he could shut the car door.

Before she made it all the way around, he reached out and grabbed her by the shoulder. Maya's heart pounded. Excitement surged in a rush of heat. Her eyes met his, her breath snagging in her throat at the intensity she saw in those rich, green depths.

She swallowed, loving the tingling swirls of desire sensitizing every inch of her body, but just a little afraid that she might be playing with a fire she couldn't control.

"You forgot this," he said, his words low and a little husky. Good. He was as affected as she was. Slowly, she lowered her gaze to his hand. "The goody bag of leftover chocolate cake."

"Bring it on up," Maya suggested, stepping out of his hold. "We'll share it."

Without needing to check, she knew his eyes were locked on her as she made her way up the cobblestone walkway. She put a little extra body English into the sway of her hips and the toss of her hair, then waited on the wraparound porch for him to open the wide French doors.

Hand in hand, they crossed the lobby.

"Good evening," Mr. Hamilton, the innkeeper, greeted. "I hope you had a lovely dinner with your family."

"We did, thanks," Maya murmured. Halfway up the stairs, she frowned. How had he known they were having dinner with her family? Small-town grapevine, undoubtedly. Still, she moved closer to Simon. She didn't know why, but Ham had always kind of creeped her out.

Distracted by that thought, it wasn't until they reached the upstairs landing that Maya realized Simon had won their little game in the car. He'd totally sidestepped her question, and in doing so, proved that he actually was the one in control.

She cast a long, considering look over her shoulder. Meeting Simon's eyes, she ran her fingers through her curls and gave him a sultry, inviting smile.

His foot snagged on the antique carpet runner, making him hop a little to regain his balance.

Pressing her lips together to keep from laughing, Maya turned back around and finished her hip-swaying journey toward her room. Once there, she turned to face Simon. He had a wary look in his eyes, like a guy waiting for someone to pull a gun on him. Good.

Maya leaned forward and brushed a barely there kiss over his cheek. Pulling her old-fashioned skeleton key out of her bag, she inserted it in the door and looked back at Simon.

He'd gone from watching for her to pull a gun to looking like he was waiting for the shot.

"Sweet dreams," she murmured.

There. That should clarify the control issue.

6

Simon stared at the closed door. Part of him, a part so rarely let out that it was probably covered in mold, wanted to toss aside the case. To totally forget his plan of getting close enough to Tobias to gain entry to the guy's life, house and motorcycle shop. It wanted to pound that door open. The other part, the one always in control, struggled to reel himself back in.

He forced himself to turn away and, with leaden feet, headed to the next door and his own room. Inside, he leaned against the door and closed his eyes. What a night. Drama, comedy and the discomfort of spending it all in a state of sexual frustration. Good times.

Opening his eyes, he scanned the room out of habit. Not that he expected any problems. The room was the epitome of rustic plush. A thick down comforter and a pile of welcoming pillows decorated the polished four-poster bed. A matching walnut dresser spanned the length of the moonlit window and watercolors by local artists graced the walls. Opposite Simon was a door connecting to Maya's room.

His body tensed and he'd taken two steps toward that door before he yanked himself back. It practically glowed in neon, screaming *temptation's trap, just a knock away.*

Simon forced himself to look away. He busied himself checking his luggage, crouching down to skim his fingers under the dresser where he'd hidden his gun case.

Still there.

His gaze slid to the door again.

What could it hurt to knock? Maybe see if she wanted to hang out a little? Pick up the flirting where they'd left off in the car and see where things went?

No. He was on the job. A job in which he'd already lied to her once. He'd have to be a total dick to try and seduce her under these circumstances.

Suck it up, Barton, he thought. *She's off-limits.*

Ignoring his body's furious protests, he emptied his pockets then used his cell phone to check emails. Other than junk, there was one from Hunter reminding him that he was reassigned and to check in daily until he'd reported for duty.

Simon cast a quick glance at the window, then winced. Not that he was paranoid or anything, but he wouldn't be surprised to find out Hunter had tracked the GPS on his phone and would show up at any time to demand he step off the case.

Which meant he couldn't waste any time.

He still had the keys to the Honda. He'd wait until her lights were out, then give it a half hour before he went back to town. Depending on where Tobias was, home or the motorcycle shop, he'd break in and do a little recon.

Tossing his coat on the plump chair in the corner, he stripped off his shirt and draped it over his coat. Needing to do something to shake off the intense sexual tension pounding through his body, he dropped to the floor to do pushups in quick succession.

As he hit ninety, he felt a cool draft. The hairs on the back of his neck stood at attention. Turning his head, he saw two sets of bare feet standing in the doorway connecting their rooms. One set had vivid red toenails, with tiny flowers painted in the corners. The other set was covered in black-and-white fur.

His gaze traveled upward, taking in the smooth golden-skinned legs. They were about a mile long, cut off midthigh by a teeny tiny leopard-print satin nighty. He'd have to wrench his neck to get the rest of the view, so he jackknifed into standing position.

Avoiding looking at her scantily clad body while he was so scantily clad himself, Simon dove for his shirt. Before he could grab it, though, Maya's cat padded over and pounced on it.

"No need to stop on my account," Maya said, her words low and husky. "I was enjoying the show."

Simon grimaced, rubbing his hand over the cat's soft head as a pre-apology before trying to tug his shirt out from under it. The kitty rubbed her black-and-white head against his fingers, letting out a soft purring sort of meow. Then, before he could move her and get his shirt, the cat swatted at him.

"Hey!"

"Sorry. Dottie gets a little snippy sometimes."

"She almost snipped the tip of my fingers off."

"What? A big strong man like you, with all those lovely, lovely muscles..." Her words trailed off as she let her eyes trace over his bare chest, shoulders and biceps. Appreciation glowed in her golden eyes as she wet her bottom lip and sighed.

"Yeah. A big strong guy like you, I'd say you can hold your own with one tiny little kitty-cat."

Simon eyed the cat, who was staring at him through pale green eyes that just a second ago had been slitted with pleasure. Was the feline's moodiness indicative of her mistress's personality?

"I'd kinda like my shirt," he muttered, feeling like an idiot.

Not thinking, he turned to glare at the cat's owner as if she'd trained her pet to hold clothing captive.

His brain immediately short circuited.

She was gorgeous.

Black curls waved over her shoulders, teasing the tips of her satin, leopard-print-covered breasts. Her nightgown looked like a slip, with narrow straps holding up the shimmery fabric and a swath of lace highlighting the curves of her breasts. As a nod to modesty, she wore a robe of sorts. The same fabric as the nightgown, it had wide lace lapels and draped low, hanging from the edge of her shoulders to the floor as if gravity were trying to torture him.

"I think Dottie would prefer to keep it for herself," Maya said, laughing a little. She sent the cat a look of approval.

Feeling ganged up on, and half-naked, Simon shoved both hands in the front pocket of his jeans. He didn't mind the ganging up. He could hold his own, regardless of numbers.

But the half-naked part? Not conducive to keeping his hands off Maya. Especially when she was looking at him like he was a hot fudge sundae and she had a desperate urge to play in the whipped cream.

"Look," he said, not sure where he was going but knowing it couldn't be where he wanted. "I'm pretty worn out. Early start, long drive. You know, busy day with meeting your family and trying to convince your brother that a polygraph wasn't necessary for dating his sister."

Her lips twitched, but she didn't say anything. She just shifted to lean one bare—oh, God, the robe had slipped down—shoulder against the doorframe and arched her brow.

"Afraid of sharing your secrets?" she teased.

"Considering one of my secrets is that we are in a fake relationship, here to keep your family off your back? I'd say sharing is ill-advised, wouldn't you?"

"Actually, that'd be my secret." She gave him an amused

look, but he could see the tension in her eyes, as if she had a few other secrets, too. Juicier secrets.

Secrets that might bring her father down? Something to consider. But Simon had managed his career to date without having to use his body and he wasn't about to start now. A key point, since he had a strong suspicion that at some point, between him and Maya, there would be bodies involved.

"Regardless, I think it'd be better for both of us if we limit my time with your brother to large group settings."

"Not a bad idea," she agreed, straightening from the door-frame and stepping farther into the room. Simon tensed, his body on full alert. This was a bad idea. She shouldn't be in here. Not with him half-naked and her looking so freaking gorgeous.

"I was lonely," she said quietly. Her smile dimmed a little and the stress of the evening's events was clear on her pretty face. "Too many memories, too much to think about."

"I can't imagine how hard it would be to see family again after so long."

"Harder than I thought," she acknowledged. "I knew it would be rough to come home, but I didn't realize it'd make me miss...them."

Them was clearly her father. Simon's father had walked out so early in his life that he'd never been real enough to actually miss. But Maya's pain was coming through loud and clear. Fatherless, he had no idea what a tight relationship with a parent felt like, let alone the loss of one. But if the look on her face was anything to go by, it pretty much sucked.

"I'd imagine there's not a whole lot more devastating than a rift between daddy and his little girl?"

"Daddy's girl?" she said with a tearful laugh. "Did you know that was my nickname growing up? I haven't heard that term in, well, forever."

Then, as if consciously breaking off the weepy emotions,

she gave him a bright smile. "But hey, as we clearly saw to-night, daddy has a new girl. Right?"

"She's nothing. Not compared to you. I'm sure your father feels the same. Maybe if you talk to him, he'll tell you just that."

"You're so sweet," she said with a smile. "I knew coming in here would make me feel better. I'll bet I could feel even better, though. Don't you think?"

It took all of his willpower to keep his gaze locked on her face. Not because he was trying to respect her privacy or anything. But because he knew if he looked, he'd have to touch. His fingers ached with the need to trail over her skin, to see if it was as soft, as silky as he'd imagined. To bury his mouth in the delicate curve of her neck, to envelope himself in the delicious scent of that glorious hair.

Bad idea, Barton. Seriously bad.

"Sure. But maybe we should go downstairs? I saw a nice library we could relax in," he said. He tried for his shirt again, but the cat gave him an ugly look, like she was on a mission for her mistress to keep him half-clothed and she wasn't afraid to use violence.

"I have another idea," Maya said. She gave a tiny shrug and her robe fell from her shoulders. A loaded gun couldn't have kept his gaze from following its path. Down those sinuous arms. The leopard print caught on her delicate wrists, and with a quick flick of her fingers, puddled around her bare feet.

For a breathless second, he stared at those red-tipped toes.

And knew he was lost. But dammit, he wasn't going down without a fight.

And just thinking that put so many delicious images in his head.

"This isn't a good idea," he told her, truly regretting the words he was about to use to try and push her away. "I don't want to take advantage of you when you're vulnerable like this."

"Take advantage?" She gave an incredulous laugh, waving that away like she had no clue what he meant. "I came to you, Simon. I'm not doing anything I don't totally want to do."

"Look, Maya—"

Before he could finish his thought—before he even knew what he was going to say—she took two steps forward, bringing her body within touching distance of his.

The scent of her, night-spiced flowers, wrapped around him like a hypnotic spell. Her eyes were wide, lashes so thick and lush they brushed her brows as she looked up at him. She wet her lips, the sight of her pink tongue making Simon's body harden painfully.

Maya stepped away, stopping right next to the fluffy down comforter turned down on his four-poster bed. The distance should have given his brain breathing room to function.

But it didn't.

Her eyes holding his, she traced her fingers over the lacy edge of her nighty. Her nails scraped gently, just enough to leave a faint red trail from her cleavage to the tiny strap on her shoulder.

Her lashes swept down, just for a second. A warning? Then, one brow arched, she met Simon's eyes again. Her lips quirked in a teasing smile.

And she pushed down the strap.

Simon tried to swallow, but his mouth was as dry as the Sahara.

Her hand still poised on her shoulder, she reached up with the other and pushed the opposite strap down. Now that tiny piece of leopard print fabric protecting her modesty was only held up by her arms, crossed over her breasts.

"Wait," he protested. If she dropped those arms, he'd be lost. His heart pounded, hoping she'd ignore him. Desperate to taste her, to see her. To see how incredible she'd feel under his body.

"You don't want me to wait," she said, her words low and amused. "You just want me."

Hell, yeah, he did. Desperate, Simon strode over. He skimmed both hands up her arms, to the delicate straps. His fingers caught the fabric, pulling it back up to safety.

He'd diffused a bomb once. He'd had this same rush of energy, like a tidal wave, crashing over him. The sure knowledge that he'd just escaped his life changing forever.

Only when he'd stepped away from the bomb, he'd been glad.

Now? Now his entire body protested, with his dick screaming the loudest furious complaints.

"Gotcha," she said with a grin, shifting her arms so they twined sinuously around his shoulders. Her fingers scraped again, this time over the back of his neck. The move sent a hot shaft of energy straight through his body. Exciting energy. Turned-on energy. *Please, I'm begging you, let-me-have-you-now energy.*

Maya stood on tiptoe, leaning her body into his for balance as she pulled his mouth down to hers. Her lips moved over his, soft and sweet, like a siren luring him to his heavenly doom. He couldn't resist the invitation. He swept his tongue over her full lower lip, then when she gave a purring moan of approval, he slipped it between hers. Gently. Carefully. As if she were just as volatile as that bomb.

Somewhere in the back of his mind, he knew this was stupid. Crazy. At worst, he was putting his career in jeopardy. At best, he could be banned from the case.

Then she swirled her tongue around his. Gently, she sucked. His erection, already clamoring for attention, grew painful.

Oh, God. He was in so much trouble. As he lost himself

in the warm sweetness of her mouth, he knew he was going to pay for this later. And he knew, whatever the price, it'd be worth it.

Because his dick? It was singing a happy tune.

MAYA WAS MELTING. HER body was one big, molten puddle of lust, vibrating in time with the movements of Simon's mouth.

Oh, baby. He tasted so good. Felt so incredible. She skimmed her fingers over the planes of his chest, reveling in the smooth power, the warm strength of his body. Pressing herself tighter against that strength, she moaned as the tips of her breasts pressed, oh so gently, into his chest.

More.

She wanted more. She needed more.

He was everything right now. The perfect distraction, the answer to all of her problems. And best of all, a damned good kisser.

Now to find out what else he was damned good at.

Before she could get to exploring, though, he shifted the kiss and he pulled away. He was nice about it. Gentle, even, as he released her lips and, his hands firm on her shoulders, he set her away. And points to him, he didn't trip over his own feet as he scurried backward a safe, untouchable, four steps back.

"I'm sorry," he said, his magnolia-laced accent caressing the words. "I shouldn't have taken advantage."

Maya rolled her eyes. "What advantage? I kissed you."

"Yes, well…" He grimaced, then jerked one shoulder in a quick shrug. "I was trying to be polite."

Stung, Maya sucked in her lower lip and slapped her arms over her chest to glare. Polite, hell? He and his tongue had been totally involved there.

"Are you saying you don't want me?"

Not sure if she wanted to cry over the humiliation of rejection or the sexual frustration coursing through her, Maya lifted her chin.

"Well?" she demanded.

He pulled a face, then showing more frustration than she'd seen from him in their short association, he shoved both hands through his hair. Blond strands spiked up all over, giving him an edgy look that went nicely with the intense look in his eyes and the gorgeous sexiness of his bare chest.

"All I'm saying is that I'm not so sure that having sex as some twisted revenge against your father is a good idea," he protested.

Frustration flamed into fury. Her pout turned into a glare.

"As far as I can see, there are only two people in this room," she pointed out.

"Maya…"

"Simon," she interrupted, slashing an angry hand to cut him off. She didn't need to hear that crap. She'd come in here to forget about her father, dammit. Not to get revenge.

And she'd be damned if she'd be denied that much-needed oblivion. If Simon didn't want her, that was one thing. But to say no because he was trying to be some kind of emotional white knight? Nope. If he wanted to turn her down, he'd have to do a much better job than that.

Holding his eyes captive with hers, Maya tilted her head so her hair tumbled in a mass of silken curls over her shoulders and chest. Then she reached up, and with a quick flick of her fingers, she sent the straps of her nighty sliding down her arms. With them went the rest of the nighty, so it caught at her waist.

Simon's eyes were dilated so that the green was barely visible. Instead he looked like a starving man facing an all-night buffet. And all he had to do was reach out and fill himself to satisfaction. He held her gaze for another full second, then let his eyes drop.

The look in his eyes, hot and needy, made her feel sexy. And made it much easier to ignore the warning bells ringing in the back of her head.

Bells that warned that this step was bigger than she thought. That it'd change things, and shift control in ways she'd never be able to overcome.

She didn't care.

She wanted Simon.

She needed him.

"Well?" she challenged.

Simon slowly slid his gaze back up the length of her suddenly super-sensitized body. It was like he'd touched her, teasing and heating her skin with the softest of caresses.

His eyes met hers and he arched one brow and gave a shrug she knew was meant to look casual. She tried to hide her grin, though. Because the bulge behind his zipper wasn't the only thing that was obviously stiff.

"But who am I to tell you how to handle your family issues?" Simon said quietly. "You want revenge, I'm your man."

Laughing at both his words, and the teasing look on his face, Maya stepped forward. The sway of her hips released the silky leopard print fabric from her hips. It hit the floor with a whispered swoosh. She just kept walking, stepping out of it like there was nothing to the idea of prancing mostly naked across a room to throw herself at a man.

The clicking sound of Simon trying not to swallow his tongue was gratifying. Reaching him, she slid her hands up his arms, from wrist to those oh-so-heavenly shoulders. Then, gently teasing, she scraped her nails down the bare deliciousness of his chest, over a six-pack that made her want to weep in appreciation, to his belt.

"It seems one of us is a little overdressed," she whispered. Excitement with its sharp needy edges took hold. It was strong enough, powerful enough, to push away all her stress. All she could think about now, all she could feel, was the pleasure Simon offered her.

"Yeah, whatever," was all he said as he shoved his hands into her hair and, almost lifting as he supported the back of her head, he lowered his mouth to hers.

And ravaged it.

Oh, god, there was no other word.

Maya groaned, her mouth opening to his demand. She couldn't keep up. Tongue, teeth and lips all moved in a wild concert. Pounding, reverberating, filling her with an unquenchable need.

Her fingers dug into his shoulders as she tried to keep from falling at his feet.

Passion, hot and edgy with a dangerous helping of desperation, clawed its way through her. The only thing she still wore, tiny black satin panties, grew moist with desire.

Her nipples puckered, begging for attention. Her body sagged into the hard planes of his, knowing he'd hold her up. He had to. She couldn't do it herself.

No man had ever kissed her like this before. As if the entire sexual extravaganza were contained in just this one act.

Her brain had never, ever shut off before, either.

But it did now.

Then he turned up the heat.

His hands left her hair, skimming down her back and leaving a trail of tingling awareness behind. His fingers curved over her hips, tangling in the tiny straps of her panties. Her heart pounded. Her breath was coming in gasps as the kiss got hotter. But even as his mouth overwhelmed her, her attention, her focus was on his hands. Would he strip away that last piece of modesty? Would he like what he saw? Was he a visual kind of guy or purely kinesthetic?

His knuckles pressing lightly into her hipbones, he slid his fingers back, then forth inside that skinny piece of elastic. His fingernails traced, low on her belly. Fingertips tangled in her curls. But he didn't do more than skim. Back and forth. He was driving her crazy.

"More," she breathed against his mouth.

"Patience," he chided, his words distracted and husky as he focused on their kiss.

Maya almost laughed. Her? Patient? Never.

Time to take matters, or maybe something more interesting, into her own hands.

To tease them both, and because it was something she'd been wanting to do since the first time she'd saw him, she slid her hands around to the small of Simon's back, then pressed them lower, over his butt.

And squeezed.

Because, oh baby, he did have the nicest ass she'd ever seen.

Then she got down to business. Reaching around, her fingers curled over his straining erection, the length and hardness causing serious stress against the zipper of his jeans.

Simon growled. The sound was low and needy and sent a thrill through Maya.

She made quick work of his belt buckle, letting the leather strap dangle as she tried to work the snap of his jeans free. But the pressure against it was too much. She needed to touch him. To feel him. He needed to get these damned pants off.

Before she could issue the demand, though, he grabbed her by the waist and, not breaking their kiss, carried her backward. Her knees hit the edge of the bed. Maya gasped as Simon let go, letting her freefall to the cloud-soft cushion of the down comforter.

She bounced once, almost giggling at the swooping feeling in her tummy. Why hadn't she ever known that laughter and sex were a wickedly exciting combination?

"I'm hungry," he told her, making his intentions clear.

"Whatever happened to ladies first?" she asked, angling so her upper body was supported by her elbows, even as her legs dangled over the edge.

"You'll get your turn."

Maya's laugh rolled out, filling the room and echoing so loudly that Dottie, who'd been curled up on Simon's shirt, shot her a dirty look and jumped from the chair to stalk out of the room.

Simon dropped to his knees in front of her and lifted one foot in both of his hands. Maya struggled not to laugh as his fingers wrapped around her ticklish toes. He blew a puff of warm air over her arch and it was all she could do to keep from pulling away to avoid the razor's edge contrast of tension and unstoppable giggling.

"Having fun yet?" he teased, grinning up at her with a very sexy, very mischievous little-boy look.

"Is this supposed to be sexy?" she shot back, biting her lip and wiggling. "I might be a little more turned on if you were holding up a sleek Jimmy Choo or Manolo for me to try."

"We'll just see about that," he vowed. Then, still smiling, he winked. And pressed one damp kiss to the inside of her ankle.

Maya shivered. Laughter faded and her stomach clenched for a whole different reason. Simon nibbled tiny little kisses down her ankle and to her arch. One hand cupped her heel while the other smoothed tiny little tingly circles up her calf.

His eyes holding hers captive, he sucked her baby toe into his mouth. As he did so, he slid his fingers higher, leaving a trail of heat up the inside of her thigh. Her eyelids growing heavy with delight, Maya shifted her legs apart just a little in invitation.

A perfect Southern gentleman, he didn't refuse. As Simon's mouth moved over her toes, sucking, nibbling and teasing, his fingers curved under the tiny satin placket of her panties. He slid the finger along her thigh, coming teasingly closer to her core with each pass.

Maya scooted just a little lower on the bed, bringing her knees up, her body closer. Tempting him.

Then she hooked both thumbs into the elastic at her hips and pushed it down to her knees. Daring him.

Her eyes locked on his, she scraped her own fingers back up her thighs, pausing at the tidy black curls. His eyes left hers at that point, staring laser-sharp and hot. Even as he kept nibbling and teasing her toes, his fingers followed the path his eyes had taken, slipping between her thighs to trace her aching, swollen flesh.

Maya shuddered with pleasure as his touch sent shivers of delight through her body. His kisses started moving up her calf as his index finger circled and rubbed her clitoris. She was on fire. Her breathing sped up, in time with her racing heart. As his warm breath wafted over her now wet, swollen bud, she gripped the blankets and lifted her hips higher. Begging him.

Always the gentleman, Simon didn't make her beg for long. His breath grew hotter as his fingers shifted, sliding into her aching flesh, penetrating her very core. His tongue traced the same path his fingers had taken along her swollen bud. Softly at first, then faster. His fingers, first one, then two, pumped as his teeth nipped, his tongue soothed.

Her body tightened. Tension coiled deep in Maya's belly, her breath coming in pants as a buzzing filled her ears.

He sucked on her clit, his fingers plunging faster and faster.

The climax grabbed her so fast, she almost screamed at the power of it.

Stars, serious freaking stars, exploded behind her closed eyes. Body arched, Maya reached overhead to grip the far edge of the bed, needing something to hang on to as the orgasm took her on a wildly delicious flight.

Well, well, she thought as she slowly floated back into her body. Talk about incredible. And addicting.

Like sexy designer shoes, Simon's affect on her body was the thing obsessions were made of. And he went so much better with naked than any pair of pumps she'd ever worn.

Now to see what else he had to offer...

7

MAYA'S PURR WAS AS SEDUCTIVE as the sight of her lying there, naked and flush with satisfaction.

Had he ever tasted anything as delicious as her? From her luscious mouth to delicate little toes, she was pure decadence. Rich and sultry, she made Simon want to grovel. To beg. To do anything for just one more taste.

Swallowing hard before he admitted any of that, or worse, actually begged and lost all claim to studliness, Simon rose to his feet. Looming over her still-quivering body, he gave a satisfied smile as he noted passion's flush staining her chest and the rapid rise and fall of those glorious breasts. She didn't play the false modesty game, instead lying there in all her gorgeous glory, spread eagle on the bed, her legs dangling over the edge of the crisp cotton duvet.

All that hair, curls he couldn't wait to feel teasing his own body, splayed around in sharp contrast to the white bedding.

She gave a shuddering sigh, then slowly, with a gentle flutter of those lush lashes, her eyes opened. Her golden gaze speared him. Then a slow, wicked smile spread over her face.

"My turn," she said.

"Wasn't that your turn?"

"Oh, no," she purred. "My turn includes you, naked. Me tasting. Then us, hot and wet and wild, coming together."

Simon damn near came that very second. Gulping hard and clenching his fists to hang on to his fragile thread of control, he shook his head. "You really should work harder to overcome your shyness."

"So I've been told."

Grinning, she sat upright in one swift move. She tucked her feet under her butt, then quirked a finger. "C'mere."

"Yes, ma'am."

As soon as he was in reach, she grabbed the placket of his jeans with both hands and tugged.

"Easy there, sweetheart," he cautioned with a laugh. "We don't want to break anything."

Although he was pretty sure he was as hard as steel, which meant breaking was unlikely.

"I want these off. Now."

Simon's laughter faded at the desperate desire in her voice. He'd never had a woman so obviously want him the same way he wanted her. With a strong, powerful passion. Usually, he had to temper his needs. Play nice. Gentlemanly sex was all good and well, but he was starting to think he'd finally found a woman who could meet all his sexual needs.

Who could go hot and wild and a little dirty, and still meet his eyes in the morning.

He was pretty sure this was the biggest turn-on of his life. Until he watched Maya tug his zipper down with her teeth.

Now *this* was the biggest turn-on of his life. His new fantasy to beat.

Then she nuzzled a soft kiss low on his belly, just above the band of his boxers, and blew his contemplation all to hell. Instead, his body took over. Need pounded through him.

"Off," she murmured again, her fingers curling into the sides of his jeans. She pushed the fabric down his hips, freeing his straining erection so it stood at attention right there in front of her face.

The grin she shot him was a fabulous combination of naughty and sweet. She shoved his pants to his knees, then gently scraped her fingers back up his thighs to his clenched butt.

It wasn't manly to shudder in delight, but oh God, she made him feel good. Then, her eyes holding his, she leaned forward and blew a warm puff of air over the head of his straining dick.

Simon did shudder with pleasure then.

Her eyes narrowed, she ran just the tip of her tongue around his head. Simon groaned. His fingers dug into the silky flesh of her bare shoulders.

She sipped, lips pursed, over his flesh. Her tongue swirled. Then she sucked, just the tip. Every nerve in his body was centered right there in his very happy cock.

She ran her tongue down the length of him.

Very, very happy cock.

She took him into the wet heat of her mouth.

Simon's moan was low, his muscles tight as she sucked, swirled and sipped him into a state of overwhelmingly intense pleasure.

Her fingers slid up and down the back of his thighs, adding another dimension of delight to her ministrations. The apple scent of her hair filled his senses as he combed his fingers through her long curls. Her teeth scraped, edgy and gentle, along the length of his shaft, sending a bolt of excitement that teetered on that border between pleasure and pain.

"More," he demanded.

Before Maya ask what he wanted more of, hell, before she could even blink, he pulled away.

Slipping his hands beneath her arms, he lifted her high,

then sent her flying across the mattress. Her laughter rang out, making him smile.

Simon liked sex. He enjoyed both the simplicity and the complexity of it. And he was pretty damned good at it, if he did say so himself.

His sexual experience had never included laughter before. But watching the humor shining from Maya's golden eyes, the smile as it played over the tasty fullness of her lips, he realized he'd been missing out.

On humor. On delight.

On Maya.

But no more.

"Bouncy," she said of the bed as the mattress settled. Her smile was both amused and excited. "You sent my stomach tumbling, like a roller-coaster ride."

She lay there, her thighs barely spread, her torso at a tempting angle as she propped herself up on her elbows. Black curls tumbled over her breasts, so the deep pink nipples played a game of peek-a-boo.

His mouth watered for another taste. His body, already tense with need, was on fire for her. And for the first time in his life, his brain was as turned on as his body.

"I've got another ride in mind," he told her, sliding his fingers along her foot and watching her shiver.

"Yeah?" Using the foot he wasn't holding, she tiptoed it up his thigh, then smoothed it back down in an erotically charged caress. "What kind of ride? The kind that goes high and wild? Or low and deep?"

He almost whimpered.

God, she was fabulous.

"Why don't we find out?"

"Why don't we?"

Lifting her foot, he nibbled at her ankle, his tongue tracing the tiny rose tattooed along the outside of her foot.

"You're delicious," he said.

"How delicious?" Her question was a throaty purr, her smile a siren's call.

"So good that I'm going to have to taste every single inch of you."

"Haven't you already tasted the best part?" she teased, her fingers smoothing down her stomach in a soft caress. She stopped just short of the black curls nestled between her thighs.

Simon's mouth watered at the memory of just how incredible she had tasted. He pressed warm kisses up the inside of her calf, reveling in the smooth silky skin and lightly toned muscles.

"Touch yourself," he said, his words husky and low. He wanted to see if she'd do it. If she'd be that free and revel in her own sexuality. But mostly, he just wanted to see. And, he noted as he stared up the long length of her legs, he had the killer view from here. "I want to see you feel pleasure. Watch what makes you hot."

Maya's fingers hesitated for just a second, digging lightly into the soft flesh of her lower belly. Then, her eyes locked on his, she slid her fingers lower. She combed them through the nest of black curls.

Simon lifted her leg, draping her ankle over his shoulder as he kissed the rounded curve of her knee. His eyes were slitted with desire, finally releasing her gaze to watch her fingers trace gently over her swollen bud, so pink and wet.

"More," he whispered against the sensitive flesh of her inner thigh.

Her fingers caressed and lightly pinched her clitoris. Then she dipped one, just one, into her core and swirled it while the others still rubbed her bud.

Simon's mouth was watering as his kisses pressed higher. Close enough that the rich scent of her pleasure filled him. He lifted her other leg, gave it a quick kiss before draping that thigh over his other shoulder. She started to pull her fingers away to make room for him, but he pressed his hand against hers to stop her.

"More," he demanded.

Blowing a hot breath over her wet beauty, he pressed his hands up the sides of her waist until he reached her breasts. Cupping their heavy weight, he thumbed her nipples while watching her pleasure herself.

Maya's moves were getting jerkier. Her chest rose and fell, breath gasping. Her eyes were closed now, her chin tilted high as she seemed to focus completely, totally, on the delicious sensations moving through her body.

Simon's dick was so hard it hurt. He needed her. Desperately. But not until he drove her so crazy, she'd never think of sex again without thinking of him.

His fingers worked her nipples, twirling and tweaking until she was whimpering with need. A warm pink flush washed over her chest and her fingers were shaking.

So close.

He leaned in and sipped. Just a quick taste.

She screamed. Back arched, her body tensed as the climax rocked through her. Her fingers dropped to his shoulders, where she held tight as she rode the passion.

Crazy with need, Simon slipped her legs off his shoulders and grabbed for his toiletry bag on the chair. Two seconds later he had a condom in hand. Three seconds later he was sheathed and ready to go.

He grinned a painful sort of smile as he noted that Maya was still riding her wave.

"More," he demanded again. This time to himself.

Wanting to see, needing to commit every second of this incredible encounter to memory, he lifted her legs again and anchored her ankles on his shoulders.

Then he plunged.

She gasped. Her eyes flew open, her golden gaze foggy with the power of her last climax.

God, she was amazing.

Simon had never, ever felt anything this incredible.

Had never known anyone this incredible.

With that last thought, his mind shut down and his body took over. And pleasure became the priority.

OH, GOD. OH, GOD. OH, GOD.

Maya could barely breathe.

The climax ripped through her like a tidal wave. Tremors of delight quaked through her, one after the other, as the pleasure spun out of control.

Her body was on fire. The passion was so overwhelming Maya was almost in tears. A part of her wanted to follow the waves of the climax as they ebbed, and slide into an exhausted sleep.

But the rest of her, mostly controlled by her body, was tensing for another round. Simon was hard between her thighs. His body poised over hers, he looked like something out of a fantasy. Gorgeous and built, he looked down at her like she was the sexiest thing in the world.

Like she was his fantasy.

Which only turned her on more.

His body slid into hers in a soft, easy rhythm.

Her palms stroked the hard breadth of Simon's chest, her fingers sliding over the hard little nubs of his nipples. Her inner walls clenched him as he slipped in and out, every slide of his dick sending her higher. Making her want more.

Making her feel more.

Desire coiled tighter, low in her belly. She focused on it, needing more. Desperate to feel the release it promised. He reached between them, his fingers teasing her achingly swollen bud.

Maya's gasp was almost a scream.

Then his hard shaft plunged harder into her hot, wet heat. Throbbing and oh, so big. Oh, so deliciously big. Her body clenched around him, rising to meet his thrusts.

He plunged harder. Then slowed. Then harder again. His body tensed. Another climax shook her body just as Simon roared. The feeling of him, exploding in throbbing delight, sent her careening over the edge.

Her throat burned, she was breathing so hard. Sweat pooled at her temples and her thighs shook from tension. As the power of her orgasm rippled through her body, it sapped all of her strength, all of her energy.

Her arms fell away, but her legs still clenched tight to Simon. She wasn't ready to let go yet.

"Perfect," he whispered, pressing soft kisses over her cheeks. Then with one quick kiss to the tip of her nose, he rolled away. A quick moment to deal with the condom and flick off the light, and he was back. He pulled the blankets up over their suddenly chilled bodies and pulled her into his arms.

Maya curled in, snuggling deep beneath the cozy down comforter and gave a long, satisfied sigh.

Well, that'd been pretty freaking awesome. Never one to dismiss great sex as happenstance, she figured they were probably the best lovers to ever exist. At least, together they were.

She glanced at the window, the moonlight sparkling like glitter against the multipaned glass. There were stars out there. A whole skyful. She hadn't been raised to believe in magic, but for once she felt the need to wish on one of those pretty stars.

FREE Merchandise is 'in the Cards' for you!

Dear Reader,

We're giving away FREE MERCHANDISE!

Seriously, we'd like to reward you for reading this novel by giving you **FREE MERCHANDISE** worth over **$20**. And no purchase is necessary!

You see the Jack of Hearts sticker above? Paste that sticker in the box on the Free Merchandise Voucher inside. Return the Voucher promptly...and we'll send you valuable Free Merchandise!

Thanks again for reading one of our novels—and enjoy your Free Merchandise with our compliments!

Pam Powers

Pam Powers

P.S. Look inside to see what Free Merchandise is **"in the cards"** for you!

W

e'd like to send you two free books to introduce you to the Harlequin® Blaze® series. These books are worth over $10, but they are yours to keep absolutely FREE! We'll even send you 2 wonderful surprise gifts. You can't lose!

REMEMBER: Your Free Merchandise, consisting of **2 Free Books** and **2 Free Gifts**, is worth over $20.00! No purchase is necessary, so please send for your Free Merchandise today.

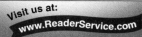

FREE MERCHANDISE VOUCHER

2 FREE
BOOKS
and
2 FREE
GIFTS

Please send my Free Merchandise, consisting of
2 Free Books and **2 Free Mystery Gifts**.
I understand that I am under no obligation to buy
anything, as explained on the back of this card.

151/351 HDL FMLT

Please Print

FIRST NAME

LAST NAME

ADDRESS

APT.#

CITY

STATE/PROV.

ZIP/POSTAL CODE

NO PURCHASE NECESSARY!

▼ Detach card and mail today. No stamp needed. ▼

© 2011 HARLEQUIN ENTERPRISES LIMITED ● and ™ are trademarks owned and used by the trademark owner and/or its licensee. Printed in the U.S.A.

H-B-01/12

The Reader Service - Here's how it works:

To wish for something special for her future. Something worth believing in.

Something like Simon.

Crazy. Just because he made her laugh and feel safe, made her go wild with need at the same time he made her feel like the strongest woman in the world? Was that enough to think they could last past this week?

Especially since this week was based on a lie.

Suddenly so sad she could cry, Maya pulled her gaze from the window and its tempting lies of hope.

"Did you ever wish on a star?" she asked. Her words were so quiet, they were almost a whisper. Not for fear of waking him. But out of nerves for sounding so fanciful.

"Sure. When I was a kid," he said, his words low against the top of her head. His hand combed through her hair, curling the tresses around his fingers then letting the silky mass fall against her shoulder before lifting it again. "For a while, I wanted to believe in anything. Stars and birthday candles. Blowing on those dandelion things. I was pretty big on hope."

Maya's heart shivered at the sound of loss in those words. She'd rarely lacked confidence, but hope? That tended to rank right up there with Santa Claus. So what made a child need that kind of promise? "How old were you when you stopped wishing?"

His fingers stilled for a second, then Simon dropped his hand around her waist, pulling her tighter against the tempting hardness of his body.

"I guess I was about eight when I realized that no amount of wishing was going to work. If I wanted changes, I'd have to make them myself."

Eight? Her shivering heart almost cried at that. "What happened to make you give up?"

"My dad walked out. He taught me not to depend on

anyone. And not to believe in anything other than what I could guarantee myself."

At a young age, Maya had mastered the three-card monte. She'd been well on her way to learning the ins and outs of computer programming, a necessity upon which to develop her hacking skills. She'd even lost her mother to the viciousness of cancer.

Hardly an innocent.

Even so, it'd been years before she'd developed that level of cynicism that Simon had discovered at eight.

She wanted to ask him what had really happened. To hear all the details so she could find a way to comfort him.

Casting her gaze back at the window, she made her wish on the brightly twinkling star.

I wish I could give Simon that hope he lost so young, she thought.

She placed her hand over his where it was curled over her waist in a silent, pseudo hug. And she swallowed back the litany of questions aching to slip off the tip of her tongue.

Nope. Couldn't go there. Because asking him to open the door to his past meant offering to open hers.

And hers was off-limits.

Especially if she wanted to keep seeing him.

And she really, really wanted to keep Simon in her life for a long, long time.

"Tonight makes me think wishes could work, though," he said, his tone lighter. As if he were making a concerted effort to shift the mood. He released her waist to reach up and move her hair aside so he could press tiny, warm kisses there, just behind her ear.

This time, Maya's shiver was for a totally different reason.

He made her feel so much. Hope for even more.

And believe, even if it was only in one tiny corner of her heart, that they had a chance.

Needing the distraction, desperate to get away from her own thoughts, Maya turned in Simon's arms. The over-sensitized tips of her breasts brushed the soft hair of his chest and a spark of heat flashed low in her belly.

Her breath caught in her chest as her body went soft with desire.

Again?

Heck yeah.

And not just because it was the perfect distraction.

"More?" she murmured as her lips skimmed over the hair-roughened planes of his face and down his throat. She breathed deep, loving the spicy rich scent of his skin. Loving even more how it blended with her own perfume so perfectly.

"You're ambitious," he said with a laugh that was just a little husky with sleep.

"Can you keep up with my ambitions?"

"Babe, I guarantee, you're keeping me up just fine."

She giggled.

Then she reached between them to test that claim for herself. "You're right. You are quite fine," she said, leaning in to whisper kisses over his mouth. He tried to take the kiss deeper, but she kept the brushes of lips and tongue light and teasing.

Fun.

Because she was pretty sure the both of them needed a little fun right now.

Something she was realizing neither had probably had much of in their lives.

8

SIMON WOKE TO A SENSATION he'd never felt before in his life. Maya was wrapped in his arms, all that glorious hair splayed over his chest and her head tucked sweetly under his chin.

And the weird sensation?

He struggled to identify it. Finally, he figured it out.

It was contentment.

It scared the hell out of him.

What had he been thinking? She was a suspect. He was using her in a case. He was here to arrest her old man. That made every single thing about this a bad idea. A horribly bad idea.

One that had felt better than anything he'd ever experienced in his life.

Obviously, he *hadn't* been thinking at all.

If he had been, he'd have spent the wee hours of the night breaking into Tobias's house, business and the three rental properties he'd discovered the man owned. Instead, he'd been doing the guy's daughter.

Freaking unbelievable.

As quickly, and as stealthily, as he could, he pulled his arm from under her shoulders and got the hell out of the bed. Time to go.

In the bathroom, he tried to gather his thoughts, his composure and, dammit, his control. By the time he'd brushed his teeth and ran a comb through his hair, he had a semblance of a plan.

Daytime B&E was out. But he was pretty sure he could still knock a few of Tobias's properties off his list of possible storage places for the stolen weapons just by doing drive-bys. He'd made contact with the suspect, had established his cover. He was in. He needed to take advantage of that fact. He just had to act professionally, utilize his training and break this case.

And keep his hands off Maya.

Simon gave a silent groan.

It was a sucky plan, but it was all he had.

He still had Maya's keys. He'd slap on some workout gear, head into town to ostensibly look for the gym he knew didn't exist. Once there, he'd check out the rentals, see if he could get into Tobias's home. Then he'd drop in to Tobias's shop, use last night's meet as an entrée.

And Maya? His gaze traveled over her form, glowing soft gold in the morning light. Her hair was a striking contrast against the white of the pillow. He recalled the feel of it trailing over his belly, down his thighs. Ruthlessly, he yanked on jeans and snapped them before things got so out of control he couldn't get the zipper up.

Because if he wasn't out of this room in five minutes or less, he knew he'd crawl back into bed with her. How much could he do before she awoke? Would she feel his kisses if they were whisper soft over her body? Would she react to his tongue if he gently licked her nipples? His fingers if they tested, teased and tormented her to a hot, wet welcome?

Crap.

Simon shook his head to clear it, then grabbed what he needed and hurried into Maya's room to finish dressing.

Dottie was curled up on the pristinely made bed, purring in her sleep. At his entrance, she opened one eye, stretched, then hopped down.

He pulled on his cowboy boots with one eye on the door and the other on that crazy cat. Last night she'd acted like she was gonna take off some skin. Now she was rubbing up against him like he was covered in catnip.

"You're as hard to figure out as your mistress, aren't you, Dottie?" he whispered, scratching his finger between the cat's furry ears.

He strode over to the antique rolltop desk and scrawled a quick note for Maya, telling her he'd gone to work out. To keep it real, he figured he'd take a quick run in the forest after he'd scoped out Tobias's place.

Then, gathering his gym bag, Maya's car keys and his coat, Simon headed for the door. He didn't let himself look at the adjoining room as he went. A smart man knew his limits.

That he was running in more ways than one didn't escape him.

"DARLING, YOU ARE THE absolute picture of your mother. Gorgeous, and so grown up now. Your hair is a little out of control, though, dear. I can make an appointment with my hairdresser while you're in town if you'd like?"

Maya was glad to turn away, both to hide her grimace and to follow the hostess to the best table at Kara's Bistro, her aunt's favorite restaurant.

"Thanks," she said as she took her seat. "But I'm happy with it the way it is."

Appearances had always been Cynthia Parker's driving force in life. Maintaining her own, demanding others change theirs to meet her specifications. Something Maya had never quite pulled off.

Cynthia Parker, on the other hand, looked nothing like

her late sister. Maya's aunt was a large, commanding woman who even in a restaurant filled with diners, seemed to be the only person in the room. Her pageboy haircut was a medium brown, with eyes to match. Once a high school yard duty monitor, she'd worked her way up the ladder of the school board and somehow ended up as mayor the year Maya had left home.

"You look wonderful, though," Maya said before her aunt could offer any more subtle critiques.

"I'm so glad I stopped by the manor this morning," Cynthia exclaimed as she took her own seat and glanced around the room as if checking to see if anyone was worthy of her time and attention. "I can't believe you were going to take a taxi into town. Didn't you bring your own vehicle?"

"A friend is using it," Maya said between clenched teeth. The furious irritation she'd woken up feeling toward Simon rose to a scary level when she glanced out the window and saw her Honda parked right there in the town square. "But lucky for me, you had stopped by to see Mr. Hamilton."

"Well, he is in charge of my upcoming campaign for state representative, dear. I try to chat with Ham at least once a week, keeping up with the local businesses and all of that," Cynthia said. "Now, tell me everything. How long are you in town? And more importantly, where on earth have you been for the past couple of years? All I have is a cell phone number. I need your address, darling. It's rude not to stay in touch, you know."

"I send Christmas cards," Maya returned, sipping her ice water and nodding to the waitress who held up a pot of coffee. Caffeine was an absolute necessity. She hadn't closed her eyes until the wee hours of the morning, and while she wasn't averse to losing a night to fabulous sex, it would have been nice to wake up for a little more.

Not that she was upset or anything. Hey, she'd learned

a long time ago not to depend on men for anything. They always, always got her hopes up, then smashed them to hell.

But a damned note? That he needed exercise? Hadn't he got a good enough cardio workout in bed? Maya had trouble swallowing past the ball of anger clogging her throat, and had to force herself to focus on her aunt.

"You and those brothers of yours." Cynthia tut-tutted. "No fault to you children, of course. I blame your father."

"Of course you do," Maya agreed. Cynthia had blamed Tobias for everything from his children's misbehavior to the way they dressed. From her sister's death to the very fact that Celia Parker had been crazy enough to fall in love with a loser like Tobias Black. Holidays had been so fun growing up.

Of course, her father had proved his sister-in-law's assessment of his character true not once, but twice. First with Greta, and now with Lilah. *The man might be clever in many ways, but he was a moron when it came to women,* Maya thought with an angry sniff.

"But we won't waste our lunch on that nonsense," Cynthia decreed. "Instead we'll catch up. Tell me everything, darling. Where are you living? Where are you working? Those little notes you send with cards say so little."

Before Maya could respond, or even decide how she wanted to respond, the waitress arrived to take their orders.

"Lunch specials," Cynthia told the girl without checking to see if Maya agreed. Then she gave a quick wave of her fingers, dismissing the waitress. Seeing the irritation in Maya's eyes, she reached over and patted her niece's hand. "I don't want to waste a moment of our time together. You said you're only here for the week, and I suppose you'll spend much of that time with your brother and his little fiancée. So this is our special time, isn't it?"

Maya bit back a sigh. Cynthia had been the only female

influence she'd had growing up. Indeed, the other woman had even tried to sue Tobias for custody at one point, sure that her sister's children needed a motherly touch. When she'd lost, she'd focused her attention on making sure Maya had a suitable feminine influence. Only her idea of influence meant touting the benefits of not wearing makeup, warnings about the evils of men and constant harping on the proper way a young lady should dress, which meant skirts to the knee, pants with no rips and heels at a maximum of a half inch.

But, as she'd always reminded Maya, it'd all been said with love.

"This is just like the old days, Aunt Cynthia. And I want to hear everything you've done since I left. I saw the new lampposts by the inn. And is the library larger?"

As always, civic duty sent her aunt into a happy litany that lasted through the salad course and halfway into their entrée.

Finally, the older woman tapped her fork on her plate, then pointed it at Maya. "Now, enough about Black Oak. Tell me about you. I never thought I'd see the day that I was glad to have my own flesh and blood far away. But with all the drama and trouble here lately, I've said more than a few thanks that you're well away from the problems your father has caused."

No surprise that Tobias was in the middle of a fracas. But what was shocking was that anyone—especially someone on the uptight side of the law like her aunt—had a clue about it. Tobias used to be so good at keeping his con life a secret. He'd taught his children the art of living with subtlety.

What was going on with him? Worry closing her throat, Maya set her fork aside and tried not to freak out too much. But this was her father. Maybe she'd given up the idea of him being invincible back when he'd let her get arrested. But she still had respect for his skills. So what had happened? What was wrong?

"Dad's in trouble?"

"He set up Jeff Kendall," Cynthia said, her tone low and angry. "Set him up to take the fall for a drug ring. A ring that he masterminded."

Shocked, she stared in horror. "Dad? Drugs? No way."

"Oh, sweetie, you've always had a blind spot when it comes to your father. All three of you did. And it's got you in trouble before, hasn't it?"

Maya shook her head. No way. Her father was a con artist. Emphasis on artist. He prided himself on his clever psychological people play, on the fact that he only targeted the rich and spoiled, and that he specialized in the unique. Mundane meant lazy to him.

And drugs, in Tobias's mind, would be mundane.

"My father might be many things," Maya said quietly, forever grateful that her aunt had no true idea of what most of those things were, "but he'd never be involved in drugs."

"Sheriff Kendall said differently."

"Sheriff Kendall was wrong."

Cynthia sighed, her eyes glistening with unshed tears, and she gave Maya a pitying look. "Sweetie, you don't understand how your father has changed in recent years. First there was that questionable relationship he had, with that horrible woman a half-dozen or so years ago. Then, without his children around, he tossed aside any sense of caution. This time, he's hoodwinked poor Caleb, tried to set up that sweet girl, Pandora. And now that you're home, I'm afraid he'll somehow involve you, too."

"Do you have proof Dad's involved?" Maya challenged, her chin jutting in a stubborn angle. She knew what her father was. But she also knew what he wasn't.

Clearly she'd come home to save him from more than just Lilah's clutches.

"Sweetie—"

"If Kendall was arrested, there must be plenty of proof

of his guilt. I know he's your friend, I remember when you campaigned for him as sheriff. But you can't pin this on Dad. That doesn't make sense."

Cynthia's smile stiffened into what Maya and her brothers had always called her political look. All teeth and arched brows, she looked like a barracuda about to feed. Then she seemed to think twice about whatever she'd wanted to say. She sighed instead, then reached across the table and patted Maya's hand.

"Well, let's just say I have inside information, sweetie. I can't share, and won't nag. But sweetie, you're my little sister's baby girl. I owe it to her, to you, to try to make sure you're okay."

And there she went on a familiar diatribe about Tobias and how he'd snuck into town, swept her sister off her feet and before Celia could think twice, she was married and pregnant.

Letting the words roll over her while she mulled worries over her father, Maya stared out the window. She saw a few people she recognized walking through the town square. Kitty corner to the restaurant, she could see Moonspun Dreams, Pandora's shop. Would her father set up a perfectly innocent woman to take the fall for his crime?

Like he'd let her fall?

But she hadn't been innocent. And she hadn't fallen, just tripped a little.

As her stomach churned the lunch special into nausea, Maya tried to breathe in calm. Letting her aunt's words fade into the background, she yanked the emotions in and focused on something, anything, outside of her father.

Like Simon. How he'd made her feel. The way he'd looked in the wee hours of the morning as the breaking sun rays had glanced over his closed eyes.

Maya's pulse skipped, but for a completely different reason

now. Her breathing slowed, her tension eased. Poor Simon, the guy had no idea that he was rapidly becoming her own personal pacifier.

And speak of the devil. A move across the street caught her attention.

Simon came striding out of Moonspun Dreams. God, he looked good. Sexy and fresh, with the light glinting off hair she'd spent a lovely number of hours running her fingers through. He had both hands tucked in the pockets of his jacket and a huge smile on his face.

And, her eyes narrowed, a slut on his arm.

Lilah was hanging all over him. Her hair teased in huge waves, her jeans so tight they had to be squishing her kidneys and her cheap drugstore heels teetering, she curled her claws around Simon's arm. Then she had the nerve to pat his bicep like it was her very own pet.

Maya's jaw clenched, her teeth sore from biting back the furious cuss words that she wanted to spew. And, she was horrified to realize, the tears she was barely keeping in check.

Stupid. He wasn't her real boyfriend. Hell, she'd paid him to play make believe. Sure, they'd had some fabulously delicious sex. But that wasn't a commitment.

The key to a good con was threefold. First, keep it simple. Second, stay on track. And third, always walk away when it was over. Always. Greed and distraction were the death knell to many a brilliant plan.

The white hot, vicious jealousy clawing at her guts could only be labeled greedy and distracting. And she needed to get over it or she'd blow the deal.

She hated this feeling. Was there anything worse than jealousy? Especially jealousy over Lilah Gomez, acting true to form and trying to steal yet another of Maya's guys away.

Being dipped in boiling oil might be worse. Having her hair ripped out by the roots. Wearing ugly shoes.

But that was about it.

So what was she going to do about it? Maya tried to get past the painful burning behind her eyes and the tight ball of misery in her belly and think.

And once her mind was clear, she'd figure out what was going on with her father. Find a way to save him from whatever mess he'd made of his life. That was her priority. It had to be.

Because clearly, counting on Simon was out of the question.

Dammit.

SIMON HAD SPENT A LOT of his life undercover. He'd worked cases that brought him into contact with the dregs of society. His average workday was spent with crooks and cons and liars. But never had any of that given him a bigger headache than he had now.

All he'd been able to think about as he drove from property to property to see if they were potential storages sites for the stolen weapons was that he was betraying Maya.

He was almost grateful for the distraction Lilah had offered when she'd practically pounced on him when he'd parked in the town square.

Almost.

"Why don't I show you the rest of the town?" she offered with a flutter of her lashes. "We even have a couple of decent restaurants, if you don't mind small-town fare."

The disdain in her tone made Simon wonder why a woman like her was still in Black Oak. It obviously wasn't town pride. And given the way she was pressing her breast against his bicep, he doubted it was love for her much older boyfriend.

Still, she could be useful.

"I did want to stop in and see Tobias's motorcycle shop. Maybe you can show me the way?"

"Of course. It's just around the corner. We can walk and talk, and you can tell me what the story is between you and Maya. Have you been dating long? Is this just a casual thing or are you serious?"

"Serious," Simon said quickly, figuring that'd get her to let go of his body. "Really serious."

Instead of letting go, though, she gave a satisfied smile and leaned in closer. "Isn't that interesting? It's kinda funny, but over the years in most of Maya's relationships I end up with her guys. I don't even try. They just sort of gravitate to me. Isn't that funny?"

Funny? That Maya had gone through high school with her best friend trying to steal her boyfriends, and now glomming on to her father? Simon looked down at the gleeful ego shining in the woman's eyes and considered all the ways he could use this.

Then, breathing in the cloying sweetness of her perfume, he decided it just wasn't worth it. He could get plenty of info through other sources. Ones that wouldn't hurt Maya.

He'd worry about the fact that his priority had shifted from climbing the career ladder to protecting Maya later.

"The bike shop is just there, around the corner. I'll give you the grand tour, okay? I'm sort of the unofficial hostess there now. Given that Tobias and I are, well, you know."

"What exactly are you?" he prodded, figuring this was one question Maya wouldn't mind him asking.

"At the moment, we're keeping company," she said with a look that made that sound the equivalent of shooting porn. "But I have a feeling we'll be a lot more soon."

Maya would love that. Simon's smile was a little sick around the edges. The only thing that kept him from grimacing was that she'd just waved her hand toward a building with a large Harley sign and three bikes parked in front of it.

"Come on in. I'll introduce you to everyone. Tobias is gone this morning, he had to make a delivery."

What kind of delivery was Tobias making? When had he changed his M.O. from cons to guns? The only way Simon was going get answers was to poke around and subtly ask the right questions.

His eyes widened when he stepped into the motorcycle shop. Whatever Tobias was doing, it was obviously paying well. The store was impressive. Huge framed prints of custom Harleys flanked the walls, interspersed with neon signs. Eight bikes, shiny and bright, were parked around the showroom floor and a long leather counter spanned one wall.

The *everyone* Lilah introduced him to turned out to be Jason, the sales manager and Lucas, the mechanic. Both, Simon estimated, in their early thirties. Jason had that pseudo edgy thing going on: a couple of trendy tattoos, a leather vest and a hundred-dollar haircut. He greeted them with a big grin and a lot of friendly chatter, looking curious about the boss's girlfriend showing up with another man, but not surprised.

"Simon is dating Toby's daughter," Lilah explained, making it sound like he was sacrificing himself for some noble cause. "She's all tied up with family stuff, so I'm playing hostess."

"Whoa, Maya's back in town? I remember her from school. She was a few years behind me, but man was she a hottie," Jason exclaimed, looking toward the large plate glass window fronting the store as if he'd see her waving outside. Then he gave Simon an appreciative grin. "Dude, nice taste."

"Thanks," Simon murmured, watching Lilah pout. "So how about you show me the rest of the place? Any cool bikes being renovated?"

Lilah had to swallow a couple of times while glaring at

Jason, but finally she jerked her head toward a door toward the back of the showroom.

Lucas wasn't as mellow about Simon's presence. Whether it was loyalty to his boss, or his own crush on Lilah, he had nothing but glares and monosyllables for them.

"Lucas is Tobias's right-hand man," Lilah said, trailing her fingers over the mechanic's shoulder as he bent to work on a bike. "He's been here for almost six months now and is a brilliant mechanic."

"Right-hand man in only six months. That's impressive."

Lucas shot Simon a glare out of the corner of his eye, then jerked his shoulder. "What's the deal? You shouldn't be bringing strange guys back here. Not with the boss away."

"Simon isn't strange. He's dating Tobias's daughter."

That worked like a stamp of approval. Lucas chilled out enough to answer Simon's random-seeming questions. In the meantime, Simon cased the room. As wide as the showroom, but twice as deep, this was clearly the heart of the operation.

Before he could do more than a visual inspection, Lilah scooted herself up on a stack of crates and swung her feet so her heels banged against the wood.

"Hey, watch it," Lucas yelped, jumping to his feet. "That stuff in there is valuable."

"Fine," she huffed with a glare. Hopping to her feet, she warned, "Don't think I'm not telling Tobias that you're being a jerk to me, though."

"Those parts are custom-ordered chrome parts and I'm on a deadline to get these bikes done. Don't think he's gonna worry that you had to sit somewhere else so I could finish on time."

Still, Simon's antenna was buzzing.

The intercom rang, then Jason's voice came over a speaker. "Lilah, we've got a customer that'd like to test ride one of the bikes. I can't get away right now. You up for showing him the route? Bring Lucas out. The guy has a lot of questions about custom features and the condition of his soft tail for a trade-in."

"Could this shop run without me?" Lilah wondered with a put-upon sigh. Then she inclined her head toward the door and gave Simon an arch look. "C'mon, it'll be fun. After I take this guy on a test ride, you can try out a bike. I'll bet you can handle a whole lot of power."

While Lucas rolled his eyes, Simon unobtrusively slipped his hand into the pocket of his jeans and pushed a button on his phone. Five seconds later, it chimed.

He made a show of pulling it out and checking the display, then grimaced and looked at the other two. "You don't mind if I take this, do you? It's important. And, you know, private."

Lilah frowned. Simon wasn't sure if it was because she didn't want to leave him alone or because she thought it might be Maya on the phone and she wanted to stir up trouble.

"Lucas!" Jason yelled.

"Don't touch anything," Lucas mumbled, wiping his hands on a red rag and tossing it toward a tall toolbox before skulking out the door.

Lilah hesitated, glancing from the door to Simon and back. Then, with a little shrug, she followed Lucas.

Simon waited, counting to ten. Then with one eye on the door they'd gone through, he stepped toward the three small crates. A pry bar lay across the top one, having been used to loosen the nails. But it didn't look like the lid had been removed yet.

His phone still tucked to his ear as if he were on an actual call, Simon shifted the lid and looked inside. Straw-colored packing material and a whole lot of chrome.

Then something darker, denser, caught his gaze.

His heart sped up. Muscles tightened and the hair on the back of his neck stood on end.

Well, well. Eyes narrowed, Simon shook his head. Talk about luck. Crazy luck. He'd hoped to find something to incriminate Black.

But this had been much easier than he'd expected.

Maybe a little too easy.

He poked his finger at the packing material, careful not to touch any of the metal and leave a fingerprint.

Packed in there between the shiny chrome mufflers and tailpipes was dense black metal. Simon glanced around, then grabbed a pencil off a nearby toolbox. A quick check toward the showroom and he could hear Lilah and Lucas laughing and talking to the customer. He hurried back to the crate, and using the pencil, he lifted one of the black pieces of metal out.

Yep.

Black really was running guns. Automatic lower receivers for what, at first glance, Simon figured was an M4 machine gun. The upper part of the gun was easily obtainable and legal. But a fully automatic lower receiver, the part that regulated whether one or forty bullets could be released at once? Totally illegal, in all fifty states. Especially California.

Knowing his time was limited, Simon poked through the packing material with the pencil, counting at least six lower receivers mixed in with motorcycle parts.

Suddenly, Lilah's voice grew louder. She was coming back. Using the pry bar, Simon lifted the metal. He tugged the sleeve of his jacket down over the fingers of his left hand and laid the receiver across the fabric, committing the serial number to memory.

Then he tossed it back in the crate, fluffed the packing straw and shifted the lid back in place. He'd just set the pry bar on top when she cleared the doorway.

"Yeah, thanks," he said into his dead phone, pacing with

his back to Lilah as if he didn't notice her return. "I'll check with Maya and see what she thinks and get back to you."

He pushed a button on his phone and slid it into his pocket, turning at the same time and making a show of being surprised to see her.

"Hi," she trilled from her perch by the door. "Did you miss me?"

Since there was no polite response, he just smiled and gestured to the window and the alley beyond. "I was checking out the fancy stained glass. Moons and suns and stars. That's Pandora's place, isn't it?"

Lilah wrinkled her nose toward the window, then shrugged. "Sure. Those are the café windows. She claims her food is an aphrodisiac. I'm not saying I believe that, but maybe it'd be a fun little experiment, hmm?"

Was she really coming on to him? Simon's ego wasn't big enough to think it was anything personal. More like a swipe at Maya. But still, she was in and out of this shop. She was tight with Tobias. And she seemed to have somewhat fluid morals. All of which meant she could probably fill him in on the guns. Like confirming where Tobias had got them, pointing the way to who they were being sold. And if rumor around town were true, what Tobias's tie-in with the recently busted drug ring was.

All good reasons to use Lilah.

Even if the very idea made him feel dirty. He almost shuddered. Dirty and disloyal.

"Sure. I was so distracted by the merchandise, I didn't even realize there was a café." He made a show of looking at his watch, then gave Lilah another charming smile. "I have to meet Maya now. But maybe tomorrow? Lunch? You can tell me what's good."

Hurrying without seeming to, Simon agreed on a time and place to meet Lilah, then he got the hell out of there.

As he walked away, his shoulders sagged. There was enough evidence to officially open the case. One phone call to Hunter and he could kick off his new assignment with the biggest bust of his career.

Then he imagined Maya's face. She might not yet realize she'd come home to make amends with her father, but he did. What kind of jerk would he be to have her father hauled off before she had a chance to heal their relationship?

Then again, maybe Tobias wasn't guilty. Maybe the rumor was true and someone had tried to set him up to take the fall in last month's drug bust. If so, it was remotely conceivable that the guns tied into that.

He owed it to Maya to double and triple check before opening a case on her father, didn't he? Otherwise, he'd be destroying any chance of this thing between the two of them becoming real.

And that was something he suddenly, desperately wanted.

9

PRETENDING SHE WASN'T furious, Maya curled up on the bed with Dottie purring a soothing tune against her side. She booted up her laptop and plugged in her internet USB, and waited for access. The Manor had wireless, but she didn't trust open modems.

As she waited for her Captain Jack Sparrow wallpaper to load, Maya stared out the window. The bumper of her car was barely visible, but it was right there where she'd parked it.

After, of course, she'd used her spare key and driven it back from the town square. Leaving Simon behind doing who knows what, who knows where, had been the most pleasure she'd had since he'd pulled his head from between her thighs this morning.

And not just because he'd taken her car and ditched her without so much as a kiss goodbye. Or that he'd made her feel like an ass when she'd gone downstairs, furious, to ask Mr. Hamilton to call her a cab and discovered her aunt visiting with the creepy innkeeper.

The fury wasn't even because of the overwhelming rumors her aunt had bombarded her with about Tobias, pushing miserable doubts and worries into Maya's head.

Nope. She was pissed because Simon was with Lilah.

Grinding her teeth against a scream of frustration, Maya punched her laptop keys to open her browser. This was stupid. She'd hired him to pretend to be her boyfriend, not to offer up his undying loyalty. So he was with Lilah. So what. Maybe the other woman would glom on to him so publically that Tobias dumped her.

As if the very idea didn't make her want to cry, Maya forced herself to focus on the matter at hand.

Hacking into her father's computers. She had to discover if her father was a dirty, lowdown drug dealer.

Even though she knew he was too smart to run anything through the business, she started with the Black Custom Rides account. Hacking into his system didn't take long.

Thirty minutes later, she'd gone through the shop's email accounts, saved and sent messages, and had glanced through the documents folder.

Now for the real nitty gritty, his accounting program.

She had to bypass two passwords, and shook her head at the ease in which she was able to access not only his books, but his bank account.

What the hell? Tobias should have better safeguards. What was he thinking, depending on a simple firewall and security program? If things were normal, she'd have lectured him first, then after a big hug, she'd have built an impenetrable wall around his system.

Blinking back tears as she imagined the scene, she felt a pang of regret, deep in her heart.

Not the point, she reminded herself. If her father was up to something, especially if it was something that would hurt Caleb, she had to find it out.

But his accounting numbers looked legit. She made a few notations to check on, especially the supply costs since they were high, but didn't seem too far out of line given the price he was asking for the bikes. Really, it looked like her father, with his usual panache, was making a huge success of his motorcycle shop. So why was Aunt Cynthia so sure he was breaking the law? Especially with something as nasty as drugs?

She'd have to do a deeper search. Home computer, secondary accounts. Because really, unless her father had hit senility along with his fiftieth birthday, he wasn't going to keep anything illegal on the company books.

Before she could do anything, though, someone pounded on her door. Maya jumped, almost sending the laptop to the floor as she exchanged a chagrined look with Dottie. She quickly closed the browser and had just lowered the computer lid when the door swung open.

"Well, well," Simon said as he strode in. He closed the door behind him with a care that belied the angry fists he'd used to announce his arrival. "Don't you look cozy?"

"I should, since it's my room," she said with a stiff smile. She hadn't expected him back this soon. In the old days, Lilah had a rep for taking a long time to please.

Her gaze as chilly as her smile, she inspected her faux boyfriend. No lipstick, no missing buttons. He looked healthy, so Lilah obviously hadn't sucked him dry or gobbled up his soul.

"You look a little uncomfy," she observed with an arched brow, noting his hair was disheveled and he had a faint glow of sweat. Had he walked all the way back to the manor? Her stomach sank a little as she wondered if that sweat was Lilah induced instead. He hadn't gotten all sweaty during their sexfest last night, but who knew what kind of crazy demands the other woman insisted on.

"Uncomfy? I just jogged five miles," Simon informed her, tossing a duffel bag on the foot of her bed. It was then that she noticed that he was wearing jogging pants instead of the jeans she'd seen him wear in town.

"Five miles is a tough run for you, hmm?"

"Five miles is a cakewalk. Five miles with a bag and jacket, that's a little more interesting."

Maya gave him a glowing smile.

"Awww, that's too bad. You should have gotten a hold of me. I'd have given you a ride," she lied, not bothering to hide her glee.

Hiding her reaction to seeing him again was harder, though. She'd brought him because he was gorgeous. Sexy and tempting, which she'd known would appeal to Lilah. Because as much as she hated the fact, Lilah did have great taste in men.

"You left me stranded," Simon accused, giving her a look that was probably supposed to be friendly but didn't hide the irritation in his eyes.

"Tit for tat," she returned, filled with both joy and satisfaction. Playing with him was almost as fun as, well, playing with him. "You left me stranded this morning."

"I left a note. You left an empty parking spot. I was worried your car had been stolen."

"It *was* stolen. By you."

Simon laughed. Then, noting the look on her face, his amusement died and he shrugged. "I had the keys, remember? Keys you handed me yourself."

Maya sniffed. Her keys weren't the only thing she was regretting handing him.

"So what's the deal?" he said, a manly smile playing around the corners of lips she'd spent that morning missing. Of course, she'd been an idiot that morning. "You're upset that I left you alone in bed? But it wasn't a reflection on our night. That was fabulous. We were fabulous together."

His voice was low and husky, the sexy tone making her toes curl and the heat pool between her thighs. He was almost as good with his voice as he was with those magic fingers.

"Like I said in the note I left for you, I was looking for a gym. I figured I'd get a day pass and work off some of the excess energy I woke with. And, to be honest, I was afraid if I stayed I'd take you again." He gave her a look that had Maya's thighs turning to mush and her heart starting to thump. Memories of him giving her that look as he was poised over her, his gorgeous body naked except for a light glinting off his muscles.

It took every bit of acting skill Maya had learned at her daddy's knee to keep the desire off her face and her breathing calm and even.

"I wanted to stay," he said quietly. And damn him, he looked like he really meant the words. "I wanted to touch you. Taste you. Slide into the warm welcome of your body. But you were asleep. It was a roller coaster of a night. The drive down. Seeing your family. Us, together. I figured you'd appreciate a little rest."

He crossed over to the bedside and brushed his fingers through the curls by her temple, giving her one of those heart-melting smiles. Her nipples perked to attention and her thighs tensed. She swallowed, unable to stop her body's Pavlovian reaction but damned if she'd let him see it.

"You shouldn't have bothered," she said, her words shaky with desire. She forced herself to think back to the image of him and Lilah, all wrapped together. That gave her the incentive she needed to tilt her head aside so his fingers dropped away. "Black Oak doesn't have a gym."

Simon's brows furrowed, but his smile didn't shift. "Yeah, I found that out. But I was there, so I figured I'd take a little tour of the town. See where you grew up, all that."

"A tour. Right." Maya arched her brow and angled her head to one side to give him an aren't-you-the-dumbass look.

"Then, after I called the sheriff to report your car missing and he assured me it was here at the manor, I jogged back."

His face tightened, lips pressed tight for a second, making Maya wish like crazy she'd heard that discussion between him and Caleb. The thought almost pulled her out of her foul mood. That must have been a doozy of a chat.

"Well, then yay. It sounds like you got your workout after all."

Simon grinned and backed up to lean his butt against the dresser and give her a long, intense look.

"So what's the deal? You're pissed because I left this morning without waking you? Or because I borrowed your car without asking?" He crossed his arms over his chest and gave her a sad sort of look, like a pouty little boy who didn't understand why he was being scolded. "I thought we were past that, Maya. I though, after you came to me last night and moved our relationship to the next level, that we at least had a little trust between us."

Oh, man. She was acting like a jealous shrew. An apology actually made it to Maya's lips, but she yanked it back just in time. Her eyes rounded and she gave him a suspicious look. Trust? He'd snuck out of bed while her body was still warm from their lovemaking. He'd stolen her car. She'd just seen him in town with Lilah hanging all over him.

Still, as a girl who'd grown up learning the art of manipulation, she had to hand it to him. That had been a masterful emotional play. And her feelings about him were still way too raw, much too vulnerable, for her to withstand that kind of manipulation.

"I'm not angry. I'm just busy," she lied, gesturing to her laptop. It was closed, with Dottie laying across it like a feline guard. "If you don't mind, I need to work for a while before we go to Caleb's engagement party."

Simon gave her a long look. Her nerves tightened as she wondered if he'd push or accept her dismissal. For all that he'd seemed easygoing when they'd first met, and even on the drive to town, she was starting to realize that was all an act.

There wasn't one thing easy about Simon Harris.

She tried to quiet the nervous nagging in the back of her mind, taunting her that she'd made a huge mistake by bringing him.

Pretending he'd already agreed to leave, Maya grabbed her laptop, sliding it from under the cat so fast Dottie didn't even open her eyes. She felt Simon stop and look back at her, but she ignored him.

Not there, she told herself. *Pretend he's not even there.* She opened her computer and clicked on a random document, pretending to read through tear-blurred eyes.

But as soon as he closed the door between their rooms, she dropped her head back against the pillow and groaned.

This was supposed to be a simple, albeit painful, trip home. Celebrate her brother's engagement, visit her hometown, save her father from a miserable relationship.

Now she was worried her brother's fiancée was conning him, hacking her father's computers and plopped right back in the same nasty competitive rivalry with her high school nemesis that she'd hated when she lived here.

But, her stomach cramped, all she could think about was what the hell was she going to do about Simon.

SIMON WAITED UNTIL HE was in his own room with the door closed before he let out a stream of violently whispered cusswords.

Pacing, he shoved one hand through his hair and tried to reel in the anger. This was ridiculous. Maya was just a means to an end. His ticket to a big promotion and the furthering of the most important thing in his life—his career.

It didn't matter if she was bent out of shape over something ridiculous. She'd get over it, or at least act like she did because she needed to keep up a pretty front for her family.

So what was the problem? She was being pissy. So what?

The what was, he admitted after his third time storming past the bed, that she'd hurt his feelings.

This was crazy. He'd lost control of the situation. Maya had an arrest record. Her father was a known criminal, wanted in eight states and under FBI investigation. He was here to build a case. Not to get so emotionally invested in a woman that he was teetering on the edge of falling for her.

Shit.

Shocked, Simon dropped to the bed and closed his eyes. Emotionally invested? Falling for her?

Where the hell had that come from?

He didn't do emotions.

And the only thing he invested in was his job.

Just because Maya inspired some weird protective instinct in him, that she made him forget why he was here and instead focus totally and completely on her? That didn't mean he was losing his edge. Then again, just an hour ago he'd made the decision to shift the focus to building a case instead of busting her father.

A nitpicky distinction, but one that he knew spoke volumes about where his commitments were.

Simon shoved his hands through his hair and frowned. No. All that proved was that he was exhausted after a night of the best sex he'd ever had. The kind that made him hard and sweaty just thinking about it.

So he and Maya were sexually compatible. That wasn't any reason to start thinking stupid. Especially emotionally stupid.

This wasn't emotions. It was simple irritation. He'd left her naked in bed, worn out after a night of count-the-orgasms pleasure. And instead of greeting him with appropriate appreciation, she'd been in a silly snit.

Knowing he needed that shower to cool off, Simon glared at the adjoining door as he stripped his shirt over his head.

Blow him off, would she? He kicked off his shoes, then stomped toward the bathroom, stripping as he went. They'd just see about that.

SIMON LOOKED AROUND the ballroom of the Black Oak Inn. Combining New Year's Eve and the engagement celebration, tonight's theme was New Beginnings. From the red rosebuds to the promise candles, the couple was clearly reveling in their future together.

The pretty people were out in force, all dressed in their New Year's Eve party-wear. Everyone was smiling and having a good ole time, which only made the miserable frustration eating at his gut worse.

He'd give anything for a quick look at that history book.

"So you're dating my niece," Her Honor, the Mayor said. Simon knew she had a name, but she'd invoked her title from the get-go of the conversation. So far she'd made sure he knew she was not only in charge of the town, she was the matriarch of the family. "I detect a Southern accent. Where are you from, Mr. Harris? And what does your family do?"

"I'm from Georgia," Simon lied with an easy smile. "My family is fifth generation banking."

"And you're in investments? Do you make a sufficient income at that?"

"I get by," he sidestepped, looking around for Maya. Or Tobias. The latter because he wanted to dig a little more, see if he could get any hint of the guy being in on the illegal lower receivers running through his shop. The former because, dammit, he missed her. Actively, physically missed her.

Maybe he was sick?

"Does Black Oak have a doctor?" he asked, interrupting the mayor's litany of reasons why the Parker family was so important to the town. Apparently to their aunt, Maya and her brothers being Blacks was merely a formality.

"Doctor?" Cynthia frowned and took an unobtrusive step backward. "There's a clinic in the next town over. A few miles past the Manor where you're staying. Are you ill?"

Simon made some random noise, which she seemed to take as agreement, since she only lasted a few more seconds before she offered a muttered excuse and left.

As soon as she did, he saw Maya on the far side of the room. She'd been blocked from view by her aunt. The knots of tension in his shoulders unraveled and Simon sighed in relief.

She was so damned gorgeous in a simple dress with sheer sleeves and an open back. The black fabric was cut high at the top and short at the bottom, highlighting legs he would give anything to feel wrapped around his shoulders again.

As if she heard his wishes, or at least his need for her, Maya glanced over. The look she gave him was far from friendly, making it clear that she wasn't through being angry with him.

But, still, she headed his way.

"You're looking a little rough around the edges," Maya observed when she rejoined him. "Not having fun?"

She didn't sound like the idea of that bothered her too much.

"Oh, sure, lots of fun. So far your brother suggested we check out the weapon upgrades he's made in the sheriff's office, your father asked me to come by tomorrow for a little lunch chat and I'm pretty sure your aunt just threatened me."

She frowned.

"You're having lunch with my father? Just the two of you?"

"Is that okay?"

Her golden eyes were wide and she pressed her lips together as she stared up at him. What was she worried about?

"Why would you want to talk with my father? That's a
really bad idea," she said, trying to sound reasonable. But
Simon caught the note of worry in her tone. Whether it was
for him, or for her father, he wasn't sure. "You're better off
keeping as much distance from him as possible. I don't want
him to know we're not a real couple. He's really good at getting information, at twisting things and getting people to do
and say things they didn't plan before they realize it."

She had a damned good handle on her old man, Simon
mused. And a bad one. Because, dammit, they were a real
couple. He just had to convince her of that.

"I'd rather you cancelled," she told him.

"I'm not easily manipulated, Maya. I can handle lunch."

"I doubt that."

"What's the big deal? It's not like I'm hiding state secrets,"
Simon lied. "Don't you trust me?"

The look on her face said duh.

His joking grin faded.

"What the hell?" he asked, genuinely shocked. Sure, he
was lying to her about who he was and what he did. Yes, he
was using her and hiding the truth. But she didn't know any
of that. So why the hell didn't she trust him?

"What's the problem?" he asked, stepping close enough
that the rich, spicy scent of her perfume drifted around him
in temptation. Giving in, he wrapped his finger around one
long, black curl and pulled her closer. "You afraid I'll let
something slip and ruin the fake lovey-dovey image of us
that you sold your family and friends?"

"Haven't you already?"

"Huh?"

He followed her gaze, seeing Tobias in his two thousand

dollar suit. And then there was Lilah, ruining that fine fabric
by clinging tightly in her zebra-striped sequins and feather
accents.

"Missing your entertainment?" she asked, sending the
other woman a sneer. "You should know that she has quite
the reputation. Better use industrial strength condoms."

"You think there's something going on between me
and your father's girlfriend?" he asked, not sure if he was
shocked again, or just horrified. He gave her a *you've-got-
to-be-kidding-me* look. But she was glaring at the couple and
didn't notice.

"Let's go," she said.

"Go where? We're supposed to stay until midnight, remember? When the happy couple will toast their future."
And when he, because they were in public, was guaranteed
another kiss from her. Since he was desperate to taste her
again, he was willing to argue if that's what it took to keep
them here.

"Please. Let's go," she said, waving the question away with
a flick of her hand. "Now. Before it gets ugly."

"Why ugly?"

"Because my father, for all his questionable taste in
women, isn't a fan of sharing. When they see us, Lilah's
going to gush all over, making a big deal out of your little
assignation together. Which will piss my father off, which
will ruin Caleb and Pandora's party." She gave him a look
that clearly said she blamed him for potentially ruining her
brother's marriage.

"Is that what this is all about?" he asked, actually shocked.
"You're really jealous?"

Looking remarkably like her cat, Maya hissed and tried to
pull away. Careful not to hurt her, he shifted his grip to her
wrist and held tight.

"Let go," she said quietly, tugging.

"Not until we settle this."

"What's to settle? We're done. We came, we attended, now we can leave."

Not until he straightened this out. Simon had no clue why, since he was basically a professional liar, but he'd be damned if he'd let Maya think he'd go straight from the delicious, welcoming warmth of her body into the arms of that tramp.

"Come with me," he insisted, taking her hand and hauling her through the patio doors.

The tiny garden was dark, except for the twinkling of fairy lights here and there. Probably they didn't figure they'd needed much illumination since it was freezing out here.

Wanting to convince her instead of turn her into a popsicle, Simon pulled Maya into his arms before she could say anything.

Once she was there, he couldn't resist. His lips took hers in a fast, hot kiss. His hands firm against her back to keep her close, he slowly pulled away and looked into her surprised face.

"And what's your point?" she asked with a chilly look. But her nipples were poking into his chest, begging for attention, and she sounded breathless, so he figured he'd already made the point.

Still…

"I'm hot for you, Maya. Like I've never been for another woman. Whatever else is going on here, whatever it is between us, this—" much to the gratitude of his straining erection, he pressed himself tighter into the warm cradle of her hips "—this is special. Whatever we're making happen here, it's special."

As soon as the words were out, Simon's inner man cringed and wanted to grab them back. What was he doing? Had he lost his mind? Words like that, they were the equivalent of a commitment or something. Insane!

Then Maya shifted. Just her hips.

His mouth went dry.

Screw insane. He wasn't blowing this.

"A man has filet mignon, beautifully prepared and waiting, he's not going to ruin his appetite with tainted beef jerky," he said quietly.

"Tainted…" Maya's eyes were as round as the moue of her mouth, then she pressed her lips tight together. That didn't stop the laughter from escaping, though.

Simon grinned.

She giggled a little more, then curled her hands around his neck, her finger weaving through his hair. "You've got an excellent point."

"I do. And I mean it. I have no interest in Lilah." At least, not sexually. But Maya didn't have to know that. "You have nothing to worry about."

To prove his point, he kissed her again. A soft, gentle sweep of his tongue over her lips. Her mouth parted, breath washing over his in invitation. He pressed deeper, swirling, plunging, taking them both on a wild ride of passion with just the touch of their mouths.

Finally, he pulled away.

"C'mon," he said, his words husky with need. "Let's get out of here. We can bring in the New Year together. Just the two of us."

He made it three steps into the ballroom when he caught a familiar sight out of the corner of his eye. His fingers still entwined with Maya's, he peered over and around the milling crowd, trying to figure out who it was.

As Caleb announced that it was time for champagne in preparation for the New Year's toast, one of the guests caught Simon's eye.

Sonofabitch.

Tension slamming through him like a bullet through flesh,

Simon automatically came to attention. His mind raced, his hand tightened around Maya's. He met the dark, sardonic gaze of the man across the room and winced.

Yeah. He was totally screwed.

And not in the deliciously pleasurable way he'd planned.

SIMON STOPPED SO FAST, Maya actually ran into the hard expanse of his back.

"Hey, I thought you were in a hurry," she teased, shifting around to nudge him with her shoulder. "What happened to all that need and want and desperation?"

Not that she was worried they were gone. Not after that kiss. Whatever this was between them, there beneath all the lies and sidestepping and games, the sexual heat was one hundred percent real.

Then she caught sight of his face.

She'd seen that look before on other faces. It was a classic *oh, shit* look.

"Simon?"

The tension running through him didn't change. Nor did he move.

"Babe? You okay?"

She looked around, trying to see what had stalled their progress toward sexual nirvana. She wanted to find it, fast, so she could kick it out of their way.

Because she really, really wanted her sexual nirvana, dammit.

She didn't see anything, though. At least, nothing worthy of slowing their progress. The partiers were shifting toward the champagne fountain. Caleb and Pandora were wrapped together in a happy kiss that distracted her enough to make her sigh.

When she'd hit a wall with her father's accounts, she'd shifted to Pandora's. Unlike her future father-in-law, Pandora wasn't an expert at guarding her books. It'd taken a whole thirty minutes for Maya to assure herself that whatever Aunt Cynthia might think, Pandora was clean.

So unless Simon was trying to scope out kissing tips, that wasn't what'd caught his attention.

"Hey, Simon," she prodded. "Weren't we in a hurry?"

"I think we'll be delayed," he muttered.

That's when she noticed the man striding toward them.

Oh, my.

He looked yummier than the chocolate fountain over on the dessert table. Tall, dark and intense, he was gorgeous with a capital G.

"Who's that?" she asked with a hum of appreciation. Not that she'd change partners for her trip to nirvana, but the view was definitely worth labeling for future reference.

"That is Hunter," Simon said, biting the words off like they tasted nasty.

"Again, who?"

"My..." He trailed off like he was coming out of a daze, then glanced at her and grimaced. "A friend."

If the tension radiating off of him was any indication, they had an interesting friendship.

"Simon," the guy said, his voice as sexy as his dark, brooding looks. "Fancy seeing you here."

"Hunter."

"I thought you were on personal time."

"I am. I'm here as Maya's date. And why, exactly, are you here?" The words were friendly enough, but there as an ugly undercurrent in Simon's tone that was a little scary.

"I'm a guest of the groom. Caleb and I were college roommates," the other man explained.

Before Maya could ask how they two of them knew each other, there was a loud chiming of dinging crystal as someone called for the toast.

"We should get together," the other man told Simon, making it sound like a suggestion when it was clearly an order. "Talk."

Maya's gaze shifted to Simon. Clearly, he'd heard the order, too. "Sure. But not now. It's almost midnight. Time to toast the happy couple and welcome in the New Year."

Hunter's brow arched. His gaze shifted to their joined hands. He gave Maya a look that felt like he'd just scanned her entire history and catalogued it for future reference. Then his gaze returned to Simon. His expression didn't change, but the room suddenly felt very dangerous.

"I really do need to go join my brother," Maya interjected before either man could say another word. Before the ugly that was simmering under the surface exploded all over her brother's party. "It was a pleasure to meet you, though."

"Likewise," Hunter murmured.

His gaze didn't leave them as they crossed the room. Maya waited until they reached the crowd surrounding Caleb and Pandora before saying, "Wow. You said he's a friend? That's odd that you would be friends with a guest of my brother's."

"Very odd. It'll give your brother and I something to talk about during the ammo tour tomorrow," Simon joked.

"Well, some friend," she said, wondering if she could talk Caleb out of being a bully. "He acts like you're a criminal or something."

Simon's laugh sounded a little choked.

10

SHIT.

Simon wanted to pace. He needed a little space and time to think. To figure out what he should do next.

But he couldn't do any of that.

Not with Maya staring at him like she was trying to delve into his brain and suck out all his secrets.

"Great party," he said, opening the front door to the inn and gesturing her ahead of him. "Your brother and his fiancée seem really happy. When is the wedding?"

"Soon, I guess. Caleb doesn't want to wait," she said, her tone just as suspicious as the look she was giving him. "So who was that man? Where do you know him from?"

"He's an…" Simon hesitated, wishing like crazy for just two private minutes so he could call, text or email Hunter and get their cover straight. "An associate."

"One of your investing clients?" she asked.

"Welcome," Mr. Hamilton greeted in a guttural voice reminiscent of Lurch from the *Addams Family*. "I hope the two of you had a lovely evening? I have wine in the parlor if you'd care to join me for a New Year's toast."

Simon narrowed his eyes. While he was grateful for the

distraction, he didn't like the way the old guy was looking at Maya. Calculating, and definitely creepy.

Maya's steps slowed, but she didn't stop. Instead she gave a casual finger wave and said, "No, thanks so much, Ham. We had enough to drink at Caleb's engagement party tonight."

Simon wondered if she realized she'd scooted closer to him. Whether Maya knew it or not, she trusted him. At least enough to want his protection against creepy old men.

"We served a nice chocolate gateau this evening," the innkeeper said to Maya's chest. "I can deliver some to your room. Personally."

"No, thanks," Simon said before Maya could respond. He wrapped his arm around her shoulders and gave the guy a chilly smile that ripped the leer right off his face. "The two of us have other things to do right now."

"Indeed," the old guy said, giving Simon a look of disdain that made it clear he thought the younger man was totally unworthy to be touching Maya. Then he turned his gaze back on her and said, "Your aunt called earlier. She'd hoped the two of you could go to the party together. I assume you met there, instead? Perhaps you'd like me to get a hold of her and arrange for a breakfast tomorrow? Or another lunch? Just the two of you?"

"Thanks, but no," Maya said with a stiff smile. Then, as if she were trying to hurry without making it obvious, she shifted toward the stairs. "I'll call my aunt tomorrow, and we'll figure something out."

"Indeed," Mr. Hamilton said, stepping aside so they could pass him to climb the staircase. Simon didn't bother to look back. He had been stared at often enough to know that the old guy watched their assent. Or, more to the point, watched Maya's.

The old guy sparked a protective streak in Simon, above and beyond the standard serve and protect. He didn't like how the man watched Maya. He was probably harmless, but Simon figured keeping him as far from her as possible couldn't hurt.

Maya didn't say anything until Simon opened the door to his room. For expediency, and just in case the innkeeper was skulking behind them, he gestured her in first.

"Not that I wanted room service, since the idea of Ham near my bed is the stuff of nightmares," Maya said, tossing her wrap on his dresser as if it were her room, too, "but dessert did sound good, didn't it?"

"Didn't you get dessert at the party?"

"No," she said, giving him a fake glare. "First you made me mad, then you dragged me out of there with the promise of something hot and sexy. Then we were toasting the happy couple, making New Year's wishes and drinking champagne. Somehow, all of that came without the delight of chocolate."

The mention of hot and sexy pushed all thoughts of Hunter, and of the creepy innkeeper, straight out of Simon's head.

"I think I have a few breath mints in my bag. Want to call that dessert?"

She rolled her eyes.

"No? Then how about we snack on each other? I'm pretty sure you taste better than any form of chocolate I've ever had," he said, walking forward to take her into his arms.

But Maya sidestepped his embrace. She gave a quick finger wiggle toward his face and said, "Oh, no. I want chocolate. It's a personal policy of mine to always welcome in the year with something delicious."

Giving him a naughty look that said she wouldn't mind including his body with that chocolate treat, she hurried across the room toward her adjoining door.

"I'd rather play a game instead," he said. Not because he didn't want to be her snack. But he didn't want her calling room service and bringing Mr. Creepy up for another leer.

"What kind of game?" she asked, pausing in the doorway to give him a curious look over her shoulder.

"How about Simon Says?" he teased. "I'm fond of that game."

Laughter gurgled, warm and inviting. Simon's grin widened. She was so damned gorgeous.

"I like the sound of that," she offered. "Are there rules?"

"Standard Simon Says rules, of course. I say, you do."

"Intriguing." She gave him a long, considering look, then shook her head. "But I want my New Year's chocolate first."

Simon sighed. Then, stiffening his shoulders, he prepared to glower at the creepy dessert delivery man.

But ten seconds, and no sound of a phone call later, Maya was back. In her hands was a large plastic container, wrapped in a purple ribbon.

"This is the dessert Cassiopeia sent back with us after the party, remember?" she said as she brought it in and set it on the tiny table by the window. Pulling a chair closer, she gestured that he grab the other one. "She said it's magic or something. It's called Four-layer Foreplay cake."

Simon was suddenly starving for dessert.

Crossing over, he pulled a chair up to the table and watched Maya unwrap the treat. "Doesn't Moonspun's cafe claim their food to be aphrodisiacs?"

Maya's grin was wicked as she pulled the lid off the box. "That's the rumor."

"Then let's get to eating."

"What about your game?"

He laughed. "Okay. Simon Says, let's eat."

Her smile dimmed a little as she looked into the box. She wrinkled her nose and poked out her lower lip. "No utensils," she realized. She gave him a questioning glance. "Don't suppose you have a fork or spoon hidden in your luggage, do you?"

He had a Glock, two knives and a 9mm hidden in various places in his luggage. But no forks.

"Nope, sorry." He eyed the rich brown chocolate, with its gooey layers of frosting between and what looked like chopped, toasted pecans along the side. "It does look good, though."

The look he offered her was pure challenge. "Don't forget, Simon Said. So you have to eat it."

Her smile flashed, both playful and naughty. As if she'd just been waiting for permission, she reached into the box and with two fingers, scooped up some of the rich, moist-looking cake.

"Well if Simon Says, then I have to obey," she agreed. Then, instead of tasting the cake herself, she held her fingers out for him.

His eyes locked on hers, Simon leaned in and took her fingers into his mouth. Rich, delicious sweetness exploded on his tongue. He wasn't a big chocolate fan, but this was probably the best thing he'd ever tasted. Other than Maya herself, of course.

"Damn," he muttered. "That's incredible."

"My turn," she urged.

He scooped up his own portion of cake and held it out to her. She took the bite, closed her eyes and gave a low groan. Then, opening them, she grabbed his wrist before he could pull it back. Holding him still, she wrapped her lips around his still chocolate-smeared fingers and sucked.

Simon almost came right then and there.

"More," he said, using the same term they'd used over and over while making love the other night.

Recognizing that he was talking about a whole lot more than cake, Maya's golden gaze darkened. She bit her lip, then licked at the bit of frosting there. He figured they'd better eat this cake damned fast, before he went insane with desire.

"We're going to get messy," she noted, glancing from the cake to his suit, then her fancy dress.

"Simon Says strip."

Her eyes widened, then her smile followed suit. Maya glanced at her fingers, then with a shrug licked them clean.

She slid sinuously to her feet, then reached around behind her to unhook whatever was holding her dress together. Turning around, she gave him a naughty look over her shoulder, then reached up and slid the zipper low.

The rasping sound, and Simon's suddenly heavy breathing, filled the room. He leaned back in his chair, ready to enjoy the show. Because there was nothing on earth as fabulous to look at as Maya, naked.

Maya shrugged one slender shoulder and the fabric slipped. She shrugged the other and it fell. Her back was bare. No bra. Simon puffed out a breath of air, glad he hadn't known that earlier. Her back still to him, she caught the bodice before things could get too interesting.

"Taking your time?" he asked.

"Anticipation is almost as delicious as that cake," she returned with a wink.

She turned, slowly. Her hand still holding her dress over the interesting parts, she tossed her hair back, then slipped one arm free of the filmy sleeve. Then the other.

Her bare arms glowing gold in the gentle light of the Tiffany lamp, Maya lowered her chin and offered a sultry, come-hither type of look. Simon obediently unfolded himself from the chair and stepped forward. Before he could get too close, though, she held out one hand.

Her tongue, so wet and pink and tempting, moistened her lower lip. Then, her eyes locked on his, she let go. With both hands outstretched at her sides, the fabric slid in a sensuous dance down her body. It puddled in a pool of black at her feet, leaving her body gorgeously bare.

Simon's gaze took a slow journey upward. Starting at
her slender feet, still wearing black high heels made all the
sexier by the ribbon wrapped around her ankle. Her legs, so
long and toned, were showcased in sheer black stockings that
ended at the top of her thighs, held up by tiny ribbons and a
garter belt.

Simon's brain stuttered.

A lacy, black garter belt.

"Oh, babe," he whispered, his words reverent.

A black satin triangle protected her modesty, so to speak,
and was the only other thing she was wearing, other than her
wicked smile.

He reached out to cup the pink tipped globes, his mouth
watering to taste her. Before he could touch that silken flesh,
though, she held up her hand again.

"Nope. Uh-uh."

"What? Why?"

"You get to play Simon Says," she told him. "But I get to
play Maya May I?"

"I love how you think," he said, laughing. He was seriously
afraid he was beginning to love every single thing about her.
"So is my game over, then?"

"Of course not. We'll take turns." She arched her brow at
his still-clothed body and tilted her head, waiting. "Well?"

Never a slacker when it came to the games, Simon asked,
"Maya May I take off my clothes?"

"Oh, yes, you may." Gloriously naked except for her panties, garter belt and those do-me shoes that were making him
want to beg, Maya gracefully sank back into the chair and
gestured that he get to it.

Ever-obedient to the demands of a gorgeous, mostly naked
woman, he got to it.

A quick shrug removed his jacket. He started to toss it on
the bed, then realized they'd be using the bed for something

a lot more interesting than holding clothes soon. So he tossed it on the dresser. His tie swiftly followed.

Nothing sexy about his shoes, so he toed them off to kick them aside, out of tripping danger.

When his fingers reached the buttons of his dress shirt, Maya started humming a sassy little stripper ditty.

Simon grinned. "I wish I had rhythm. I'd add in a little dance for you."

"Oh, no," she insisted with a shake of her head. "You just keep on getting to it. I'm happy to wait for your rhythm moves later. When we're both naked."

Looking forward to it more and more each second, Simon made quick work of his buttons. He undid the cuffs and let his shirt slide to the floor. His hands were working so fast he almost fumbled his belt, which made him stop and take a breath.

Acting like a lovesick teenager about to live out his fantasy with the head cheerleader was not going to score him any points, or impress Maya. Reeling back in his control, he forced the edgy need back.

"Don't stop now," she insisted, obviously enjoying the show. So much so that she reached over and scooped up a fingerful of cake and popped it into her mouth.

Her eyes half-mast, she gave a little moan and shivered with delight. "So good."

Screw scoring points. Simon ripped the placket of his slacks open so fast, the metal hook zinged across the room. A second to unzip and the black material and his boxers both hit the floor to join her dress.

He glanced down. His socks weren't as sexy as hers, so he tossed those aside, too.

"Oh, my," she breathed, giving him the same hungry look she'd given the cake earlier. "Don't you look tempting?"

Her eyes were as hot as a caress as they slowly traveled

the length of his body, then returned to his straining erection. She licked her lips and gave a deep sigh.

"My turn," he told her before she could suggest anything else.

"Your...?" She dragged her gaze away from his package and met his eyes. "Sorry, what? I was distracted by the view."

"My turn," he said with a grin. "Simon Says."

"Oh, right." She sounded a little disappointed, like she was ready to move on to a different game. But he had plans for this one.

He joined her at the table. He carefully scooped up just the rich frosting. Her eyes widened in anticipation. He arched one brow, then smeared the chocolate confection over the head of his dick.

"Simon Says, enjoy your dessert," he said.

"I love this game."

Still curled up in the chair, she reached out to curve her hands over his hips. Simon obediently moved forward so he was right there, in easy licking distance.

Maya gave a hum, then leaned forward. Wrapping her hair around one hand to keep it out of the way, she licked a tiny bit of the frosting away. Before she could get a good taste, though, Simon had a scary thought.

"No biting," he warned.

Her laughter gurgled. She flashed a toothy smile, then warned, "You want to play, you take your chances."

But those straight white teeth were nowhere in evidence when she leaned forward again and licked, with long slow swipes of her tongue, around the head of his throbbing dick. Then she took him into her mouth, sucking clean every bit of the sweet treat.

His blood rushing to his erection, Simon's body tensed. Her mouth had him right there on the edge between pleasure and pain. When she started licking her way down the length of him, he almost lost control.

"Wait," he gasped. She didn't stop, though. Instead she sucked him into her mouth, sliding her lips up and down in a deliciously slow, deliberate rhythm.

"Maya May I?" he groaned desperately.

Magic words.

With one last slurp and a kiss to the velvet tip of his throbbing dick, Maya gave a reluctant sigh, then leaned back in the chair.

"Yes?"

"May I have my own dessert now?" he asked.

Her pout turned into a smile.

"Yes, indeed, you may," she purred. "Shall I serve?"

"Thanks, but I'll help myself."

Taking her hand, he pulled her to her feet. He scooped more frosting, this time with just a little cake—because he did plan to nibble. Like an artist painting a canvas, he spread the decadent treat over her nipples. Then, meeting her eyes, he lifted his still-chocolaty fingers for her to lick clean.

Her eyes were so dark he could barely see the golden rim of her iris. Her breasts rose and fell as her breath, a little choppy with need, rushed through her. Simon was suddenly starving for her.

He leaned down, licking a path clean right over her hardening nipple. She gasped. Her fingers dug into his shoulders. He licked swirls around the areola, then sipped at her nipple in a gentle move almost as sweet as the cake.

She pressed her hips against his straining dick, the silk of her panties rubbing an enticing invitation over his hard flesh.

He licked the other nipple clean, then nibbled his way back and forth between the two. They were rock hard now, pouty with need.

"Simon," she groaned. "Please."

He barely remembered the condoms he'd stashed on the bedside table. Reaching over to grab one, he covered himself, then grabbed Maya again and yanked her against him. He shifted so her back was against the wall.

The panties barely made a sound when he ripped them from her body. His hands filled with the soft flesh of her butt, Simon plunged. Her legs, wrapped tight around his waist, gripped him as he pumped into her with a wild, out-of-control rhythm.

He closed his eyes, riding the wave as it climbed higher, higher, then higher still. Maya made a keening sound, then threw her head back. Her body stiffened and she let out a loud groan. That's all it took to send Simon tumbling over the edge.

His world exploded. Everything went black in his brain. The only thing real was Maya. Her body wrapped around his, filling his hands. Welcoming and milking him of every last drop of pleasure.

Dammit. He was in so much trouble, he realized as he slowly crested downward.

Because he'd fallen in love with her.

RESTING AGAINST THE wall, Maya's head was too heavy for her to lift. Her entire body had melted into one big, gooey puddle of lust.

She couldn't even open her eyes. But finally, she found enough air in her lungs to speak. "I have always loved chocolate, but my adoration for it has taken on new levels of love."

"Mmm," he murmured against her neck.

"I'm all sticky," she noted as their bodies made a sucking sound when he moved.

"Sign of a good time," he decided, still not lifting his head.

Realizing movement was up to her, Maya finally let her legs drop to the floor, then with a heavy sigh, pushed Simon away.

"Shower," she mumbled, swaying without his body to hold her up.

"Maya May I join you?"

A quick shower and a few playful gropes that led to more laughter than sex later, and Maya was curled up in the warmth of Simon's arms. Five minutes ago, they'd barely had the energy to pull the comforter over their nude bodies. But now she was wide awake.

Her emotions a tangled mess, she tried to sort through what she was feeling. Satisfaction took top billing. But coming in a close second was something she didn't recognize.

And it scared the hell out of her.

What was it? Softness, a deep, needy sort of craving for Simon, but that wasn't a surprise since he was so crave-able. But it wasn't just for sex. Or for his company, although she was having more fun with him that she'd ever had with anyone else.

Was it because he made her feel safe? That wasn't a feeling she'd had before in her life—nor had she realized she wanted it.

"What's wrong?" he murmured against her hair, his words slurry with sleep.

"Nothing."

"You got all tense. What's up?"

Had anyone in her life ever noted her emotions so clearly? If they had, they'd never cared enough to push past her defenses. Her initial reaction was to sidestep. She didn't share emotions.

Opening her mouth to do just that, she was shocked to hear herself ask, "What's the most important thing in your life?"

Suddenly his body didn't feel all relaxed and sleepy next to her. He didn't tense, but he definitely came to attention. "Most important? Besides making sure we repeat that little cake trick sometime soon?"

"Ha. No, I mean, I used to think family was the most important thing in my life. But then I left, and tried to shut that
door. And I didn't know what was important anymore."

Did that make her sound as lost as she felt? Probably. Maya
was glad it was dark so Simon couldn't see how vulnerable
she knew she looked.

"Family is important. Yours shaped you. Even if you're
estranged from them it's still obvious how strong the ties are
between all of you."

"Are you close with your family?" she asked, both because
she really was curious, and to change a subject that she didn't
know how to deal with.

"No."

"That's it? Just no?" She tilted her head back to face him,
even though the room was too dark to see his features. "Not
close because you're estranged like I am? Or not close for
some other reason?"

His hesitation was a physical thing. She was sure he would
ignore her question. But then she felt him shrug.

"My dad was gone mostly. Traveling when I was little, but
just gone by the time I was eight. He wasn't much interested
in having a family."

Eight. When he stopped having hope. Maya was suddenly
glad the dark kept her tears from showing.

"But you had your mom?"

"Sure. She was there. She spent a lot of time pissed at the
old man. I don't blame her. But all that time she spent being
pissed, it pretty much took up all her energy. What was left,
she needed to support us. She filled the hole he left with a lot
of business. Her job, her friends."

But not her son.

Maya's heart broke for that little boy, abandoned by both
parents. That he was such an amazing man, so loving and
strong, was amazing.

The upbringing he described was foreign to her. Maya barely held back a shiver, it sounded so cold and empty. So sad. Her arms tightened around his waist as if she could warm him now, and take away some of that pain.

"I think that's why my job means everything to me," he mused quietly, obviously lost in his own discovery and working it out aloud. "It's all I've got. All I have to show my worth, you know? I never felt special, or even useful, growing up. Now it's different."

Maya's heart ached for him. And for herself, because hearing how rough his upbringing had been made her realize just how lucky hers was. Thanks to her father, she'd never doubted her worth, never for a second wondered if she was special or not.

But Simon had learned to focus on the externals. That was probably why he'd gone into investments. Money was a good measuring stick.

So was love, though.

Maya had never doubted that she'd fall in love some day. That she'd feel the deep, wonderful commitment that her parents had enjoyed. But she hadn't thought it'd feel this scary.

So scary, she wasn't ready to share. Not in words. Not yet.

Maybe not for a long, long time.

So, instead, she shared in the only way she could.

With gentle kisses and soft caresses.

And while most of her was sure Simon was just enjoying the ride, a tiny part of her heart hoped he heard her vow, and that maybe, just maybe someday, he'd return her love.

11

THIS TIME, MAYA WASN'T surprised to wake up alone.

She curled into the pillow next to her, inhaling the faint scent of Simon. Earthy spice, it made her smile and giggle like a giddily deflowered virgin.

He was amazing. They were amazing together.

Afraid she was one giggle away from being a cliché, she let go of the pillow and stretched. Her satisfied body was well lubed and relaxed as it slid over the soft sheets.

She wondered briefly where Simon had gotten away to, but unlike the previous day was sure of two things.

One, he wasn't driving her car since she'd hid the keys.

And two, he wasn't having sex with Lilah since she was sure she'd worn him out. Besides, as he'd said, a man didn't go from incredible to inedible. Maya had enough faith in Simon and what was growing between them to believe he wasn't lying to her.

The bed made a tiny bounce as Dottie jumped onto the mattress and butted her head against Maya's arm. Maya obediently offered her an ear rub and asked, "What do you think of him, Dottie? I'm afraid I might be getting stupid here. Falling..."

Panic zipped through her body. Muscles tense, her stomach dropped. She couldn't even say the words.

"Distraction," she decided aloud. "I just need distraction. After the sexual glow wears off, I'll worry about the rest of this...stuff."

Distraction. Her eyes a little wild, Maya looked around the room. Her gaze landed on the drawer she'd locked her computer into and she gave a relieved sigh.

She had research to do.

Quickly, she scooted naked from the bed and grabbed her key ring from the potted fern by the window, then opened the drawer and pulled out her computer.

Back in bed, she opened her laptop and resumed the search she'd started the previous day, this time hacking into her father's private bank account and home computer.

Two minutes later, her screen froze.

A red banner flashed, then spun like a top before zooming onto the monitor.

You can do better than that, it read.

Maya couldn't help herself. She started laughing.

Then the banner changed. Her laughter faded and she sighed as tears filled her eyes.

Penalty required for poor performance.

Penalty required. Tobias hadn't been a big believer in punishment. At least, not the normal parental kind. Instead, he'd taught his kids to talk, charm or con their way out of trouble. He called it their penalty. If they succeeded, they walked away from whatever they'd done wrong. If they failed, they paid whatever price he deemed appropriate. At fourteen, Maya had backed his Ferrari into the garage door and gotten away with it with a teary-eyed story about saving a kitten who'd fallen from a tree. Another time, she'd been grounded for a month for getting a C in algebra because she hadn't studied, and had no clever excuse.

She was so busted.

An hour later, she parked in front of her childhood home. Resting both arms across the steering wheel, she inspected the three-story Victorian, with its stately trees winter bare, and the gardens she knew would be a watercolor riot of scented beauty in three months.

A painful sort of homesickness washed over her like the flu, making her a little woozy, a little weak and a whole lot nauseated. She didn't need this. Or, actually, she didn't want to need this. But coming home was making her realize just how much she really did want to do just that—come home.

As if he had special instincts, or more likely had been watching for her, Tobias swung the front door open.

Time to pay the piper.

Maya took her time leaving the car and making her way up the walkway. Both to irritate her father, who because he only wore a T-shirt with his jeans, was clearly getting cold. And because, yes, she was nervous.

"Welcome home, Pumpkin," he said when she reached the porch.

"I'm here to pay the penalty," she said, trying to act aloof as she swept past his open arms with her chin held high. "Not to play prodigal daughter makes nice."

"Well, there's certainly nothing nice about your attitude or your rudeness, now is there?" he said, after a second of standing there, arms raised. With a huff, he shut the door and gave her a chiding look. "You've been taught better manners than that, Maya."

"I've been taught so many things, father. Shall we go over the list?" she suggested, making her way down the long hallway on auto-pilot. It was the same. Six years since she'd been here, and it looked just like it had when she left.

A part of her reveled in that. Another part of her wanted to weep. She'd missed it. Missed him. She'd planned to come home, prove to herself that she was no longer Daddy's little girl. To let go of the past so she could get on with her life.

This was so not working out how she'd hoped.

"We can skip the list," Tobias said, gesturing toward his den. Maya glanced at the door where he ran his kingdom and walked right past it toward the living room. As she stepped down into the lush carpet of the sunken space, she felt like she was stepping back in time.

"You haven't changed anything," she whispered. The leather sectional was still in the same spot. The fluffy red pillows she'd picked out when she was fifteen and playing with the idea of interior design were tossed as randomly as they'd been the day she'd brought them home. The silk flower arrangements, the throw blanket, even the lopsided remote caddy Gabriel had made, they were all in the same place.

Suspicion started brewing in the back of Maya's brain. She gave the room one last look around, then turned to face her father.

"Well?" she challenged. Her chin jutted high and she crossed her arms over her chest. "What's the penalty?"

A smile played around the corners of his mouth, but he didn't call her on the juvenile defiance.

"Sit," he said.

Maya gave him a long look, but finally sank into the couch.

"Isn't this nice," he said as he took his traditional seat in the recliner. "You, back in Black Oak. Having you here, at home. Your fingers poking into my private business."

"Clumsy fingers if you caught on that fast."

"Let's just say I was watching for them."

"You knew I'd hack your accounts?"

"I suspected you'd be curious when you heard the inevitable rumors."

Maya nodded, not surprised. "And are the rumors true?

Were you involved in drugs? Are you running some dirty crime ring right here in town?"

Dark eyes met gold. Maya held her breath. For all her anger, all her big talk, he was still her father. The man who'd raised her to show respect and had once washed her mouth out with soap for smarting off. She swallowed, hard, suddenly tasting the acrid flavor of Ivory on her tongue.

Then Tobias inclined his head. Either because he figured it was a legit question. Or because he read her mind and was glad she'd remembered the pecking order here.

"You know the rules, Pumpkin. Never dirty your own nest. Black Oak is sacred. It's supposed to stay clean."

Legit question, it was. More relieved than she'd admit aloud, Maya finally relaxed. She curled her feet under her tush and pulled a pillow onto her lap to play with the fur. "Someone is setting you up?"

"You're quick." His smile was filled with the same pride he'd shown when she'd won the regional spelling championship and when she'd hacked the account of a known pedophile in the neighboring town and stolen her first ten thousand. "Yes, it's a setup. I wasn't sure at first if it was directed at me or just happenstance. But after Caleb arrested that useless Jeff Kendall, it became pretty clear that something bigger is going on."

Maya pressed her lips together as her mind raced. She didn't want to care. But someone was out to get her father. And while it was one thing for her to harbor resentment and anger toward him, it was something else entirely for someone to try and set him up. Tiny flames of fury started licking their way through her system.

Sure, they'd grown up with an *us against them* mindset as their father taught them to play the game, and play to win. But the us was always the family. And the them was everyone else. Now, a them was threatening one of Maya's own us, which meant her own feelings and issues didn't matter. When threatened, what mattered was what always mattered—protecting family.

"Caleb came home to help you out?" she asked, more for confirmation than because she had doubts.

"Actually, I'm pretty sure your brother came home to bust me," Tobias said, that same wicked grin he'd handed on to his children flashing. "He ended up arresting the good sheriff instead."

"Does he know the rest? That you're being set up?"

"Your brother is a smart man."

Her head tilting to one side, Maya gave her father a long look. He wasn't telling her everything. But what was coming through was a hint of hurt. Whether because Caleb had come home to *bust* him, or because there was still a rift between the two, she didn't know.

But she planned to find out.

"That's not why he's sticking around, of course," her father went on to say. "I'm sure he'd have walked after the arrest, considered the case closed, if not for Pandora."

There it was again. That hurt, clear in his eyes. Maya frowned. She knew that despite his need for the con and all of his tricky ways, Tobias Black loved his kids. He'd fought to keep them when it'd have been easy to walk away. And all three had turned on him when he'd made his first major mistake.

Of course, given that the mistake had been a slap in all of their faces in the form of that bitch Greta, it wasn't much of a surprise that he'd gotten the reaction he did.

He couldn't have been shocked when all three of his children had turned their backs on him.

Tears in her eyes, Maya had to look away. Blinking, her gaze landed on the large painting of the family over the mantel. The gilt of the frame was at odds with the casual setting, a picnic in the woods. Celia Black's smile showed her pride in the family surrounding her. Her boys on either side, baby Maya on her lap and Tobias, his arm protectively curled around her shoulder. Maya had missed her mother, but never felt like she was completely gone because Tobias had spent his children's lives keeping her memory alive.

"We can figure this out," she murmured.

"You're planning to help me?" he asked, sounding surprised. But there was a look in his eyes, a calculation, that made Maya think he'd gambled on just this response.

Seeing that look, she hesitated. Her stomach clenched and she sucked in a deep breath, trying to keep her chin from quivering. Did helping mean forgiving?

"I don't know," she said in a low whisper. She stopped and swallowed, trying to get the words past the lump in her throat. "I really haven't gotten over what happened the last time I tried to help you."

There. It was out in the open. Not that it'd ever been in the dark. But, before, she'd always walked away when Tobias wanted to discuss the con-gone-wrong. Her arrest. His fall from grace in her eyes and her heart.

"What would you have had me do, Maya? Join you in jail? Or complete the transaction, clear the evidence and ensure your release?"

She'd have had him plan the job better. She wished he could have pulled it with his usual panache, instead of partnering up with that conniving tramp who'd used him, used them, then left them all to hang. She'd have liked him to have warned her that the guy they were conning out of a rare piece of art had made a deal with the cops. She'd have had him rush in and rescue her before she'd had to spend the night in that cold, nasty cell.

She'd have had him be infallible, instead of human.

Heart pounding with confusion, Maya rose and headed for the steps.

"You're leaving?"

His disappointment was tangible. The hurt beneath it almost made her miss a step, but Maya managed to keep going. With a deep breath, she looked over her shoulder when she reached the hall and shrugged.

"I'm going to talk to Caleb." She hesitated, then arched one brow. "Chances are, he's already working the case himself. Better to know what he knows than to waste time trying to duplicate his investigation."

Tobias nodded. In his eyes was the unspoken question: Did she forgive him?

But she didn't have an answer.

Not yet.

"Do I need to bother listing the regulations you've violated? The rules you've broken?" Hunter leaned back in the vinyl booth of the truck stop, his look both penetrating and distant. Five miles out of Black Oak, the place was filled with truckers and travelers, all focused on food. "The fact that you've disappointed me and jeopardized your career?"

Simon stared back at Hunter, calculating the odds of getting out of this without being written up, sanctioned or demoted. It would all come down to how he handled the next two minutes.

"I'm pretty sure the rules and regs are still intact since I'm on vacation, and didn't utilize any federal resources while on my break."

"Were you aware that Maya Black was the daughter of a suspect in an ongoing investigation?"

"Were you aware that you're asking me questions that you already know the answer to?"

"Were you planning to pitch a reasonable excuse, Barton or just planning to play dumb?"

Simon's lips twitched. "Could I get away with playing dumb?"

"Nope."

A waitress with hair almost as wide as she was tall passed by and held up one finger to indicate she'd be with them in minute.

"Then I'll pitch this. I saw an opportunity to make contact with Maya Black. Following protocol I used one of my standard identities in case we needed to use the connection in the future. When she invited me here for the week, I seized the opportunity as it was made available. Since I was on vacation, I didn't see the harm in following up on my own time."

"You entered the vicinity of a known suspect without reporting your intentions to your superior."

"I think I'm going to play the vacation card again."

Hunter just stared.

Simon waited a beat, then huffed out a breath. "Okay, fine, I knew I was skirting the line. But I didn't step over it."

One brow arched, Hunter waited.

Thankfully the waitress showed up with a coffeepot. They both declined ordering, so she filled their ceramic mugs and was on her way.

"So I made contact with her," Simon said with a shrug after sipping his coffee. "She needed someone to come home with her so she didn't lose face, so I made myself available. Once here, I used her connections to get into Tobias Black's bike shop."

"How much contact have you had with Black himself?"

"Surprisingly little. The estrangement between he and his daughter is pretty deep. His girlfriend gave me the shop tour. He hesitated. He didn't want Maya hurt. Hell, at this point he'd do whatever he could to prove Tobias's innocence rather than his guilt. But Simon couldn't lie. Not directly to Hunter's face. All he could do was hope that the director's friendship with Maya's brother was strong enough that he'd go along with Simon's plan to gather all the facts before making any moves toward Tobias Black.

"While there, I noted a suspicious crate. The opportunity arose to check it out, and I took it."

Hunter had two brows up now and a look that was either anger or curiosity lurking in his eyes.

"The crate was filled with bike parts." Simon paused, then inclined his head. "And guns. Lower receivers for automatic weapons, actually."

Hunter's gaze narrowed in calculation. After a few seconds, he inclined his head.

"Nice job not stepping over that line," he murmured, finally taking a sip of his coffee.

Simon grimaced.

"I only saw one piece, but got a solid look. Do you want the serial number?"

Hunter reached into the inside pocket of his jacket and pulled out a pad of paper and pen. The man was like Houdini in a Boy Scout uniform. Always prepared.

"How many weapons did you see?"

"I estimate half a dozen lower receivers in the one crate. There were three crates there yesterday and I saw another dozen delivered this morning. I have no idea if all of them carry stolen goods or just that one crate."

"Did you note any of the crates leaving the shop?"

"Not the same crates. I did see a stack of boxes being loaded into the back of a car, though."

"Plate number?"

Simon took the pen and jotted that down underneath the serial number.

"When were you going to call this in?"

"Today."

Hunter just stared.

Simon shrugged.

"Seriously. Today. I couldn't go further without authorization." Then, in the spirit of honesty, he added, "And I need access to company resources *before* I can go any further."

"*If* you go any further."

What a freaking time to find someone that mattered more than his career. Just when that very career was on the verge of skyrocketing. But he wasn't leaving. No way, no how, would he desert Maya.

Hoping he wouldn't have to make the choice between her and his career, Simon shook his head and bluffed, "I'm here, my cover is established and I broke the case. You're not going to pull me."

Hunter gave him a long, considering look. Then, leaning both elbows on the Formica table he leaned forward and said quietly, "You're interfering in an ongoing case, in which we already have people established and are close to closing. Your presence here upsets a carefully orchestrated balance."

Shit. Simon's stomach sank as he noted the seriousness of both Hunter's look and his tone. The guy wasn't bullshitting. Ambition fit Simon like a second skin, but right this second, it was pinching uncomfortably.

"You intruded without authorization. You jeopardized our position. And when you came across evidence that is relevant to the case, instead of contacting your superior, you chose to keep it to yourself." Hunter ticked off the list of transgressions as if he was reading a recipe. "So tell me why I shouldn't send you back to Savannah in disgrace with a disciplinary letter in your file?"

For a morning that'd started with incredibly hot sex and a great mood, this day was sure going to hell.

"You're not that much of a hardass, Hunter. You're pissed

at me, but you can see the advantages to leaving me in place."
At least, Simon hoped like hell he could see them. A tickling
of panic was making its way up his spine. He swallowed hard,
trying to get past the dread obstructing his throat.

"C'mon, Hunter," he said quietly. "I didn't blow anything
and I didn't break the rules. Yes, I didn't follow protocol, but
I had a good reason."

"Which is?"

Simon hesitated. He looked into the dark eyes of the man
who was a legend. A man he'd spent years looking up to, even
though they were the same age. A man who was his boss and
held the future of his career in his hands.

"I was worried about Maya," Simon admitted. "She's innocent in all of this. I didn't want to see her hurt, didn't want
to do anything that could send this tipping the wrong way. I
wanted to get the facts first."

"And?"

Simon frowned.

"Report, Barton."

Ahh. Simon nodded and shifted in the vinyl seat. Shoulders back, chin high, he came to attention.

"Illegal, most likely stolen fully automatic lower receivers are being run through Black Custom Bikes. There is no
proof that Tobias Black is behind it. It could just as easily be
one of his employees or his girlfriend."

Hunter nodded for Simon to continue.

"Tobias Black appears to be solvent, and the real town
leader. The mayor has nothing good to say about him, but
that's most likely a familial issue. Given his history and talents, running guns, just like running drugs, would be a major
step outside his usual M.O."

That was as much opinion as fact, but Hunter just nodded.

"He employs three people. Two salesmen and a mechanic.
His girlfriend appears to be an unpaid helper. About the same

time the drug accusations started, he began dating said girl-friend, who is his own daughter's age. That doesn't speak to the crime itself, except that from what I've heard, he's only dated once since his wife died twenty-some years ago. That liaison exploded after destroying his relationship with his children and he vowed to stay single."

"You think the girlfriend is involved? Or working for him?"

"I think she's a problem and that she has an agenda that has nothing to do with dating a guy twice her age."

Hunter nodded again, this time relaxing enough to take a drink of his coffee.

"Caleb Black is a question mark. He conveniently stepped into the sheriff's job after arresting the man who previously held that position. He's hiding things, but doesn't have a crim-inal vibe. There's tension between him and his father, just as there is between Tobias and Maya."

"And Maya Black?"

"Is innocent."

Hunter's brow rose and he slowly set the coffee cup back on the table.

"There's no reason to suspect otherwise," Simon defended.

"There's *always* reason for suspicion," Hunter returned. "Of anyone."

Simon agreed. At least, he'd agreed before he'd met Maya. But now he knew her. He believed in her. And in her inno-cence.

His feelings must have shown on his face, which was dis-concerting to say the least. Because Hunter gave him a long, pitying sort of look then shook his head.

"A week ago someone reminded me that Maya Black had a criminal record. And that was reason enough to hold her under suspicion, to believe she was culpable and should be under surveillance. Ringing any bells for you?"

Simon grimaced.

"You've lost objectivity, Barton."

Simon's grimace turned to panic.

"Pulling me would be a mistake. My cover is solid. You know it's solid, or whoever you have on the inside would have taken me out already. Let me close this case."

"You're not on this case."

The hell he'd be booted out. He was the one who'd found the guns. He'd made contact with all of the players, had a solid cover. And more importantly, he wasn't leaving Maya. Not like this. Tapping one finger on the table, Simon didn't say a word, though. He just leaned back and waited.

Thankfully, Hunter wasn't big on playing head games. After a painfully long minute, he nodded.

"You're on backup," Hunter decreed, sliding from the booth. "Wait for orders, keep guard on Maya Black, and watch your ass. If you see a chance to break this case, you take it. Regardless of how it'll affect whatever it is that isn't going on between you and the daughter of a suspect."

He stood next to the table, waiting. Watching.

Testing.

Simon forced himself to shut up and wait.

"If you stay on my team, you'll find out that I'm not a stickler for protocol. But I'm adamant about loyalty."

Working with Hunter, being on his team, was a huge career leap. The man's reputation was legend in the FBI.

"You won't question my loyalty again," Simon promised.

Hunter nodded and without another word, left.

Simon swigged down the last of his coffee.

He'd fucked up. Simon stared out the window blankly, thinking of all the reasons he loved his career. His job was his life. Everything he was came down to what he did. And he'd worked hard to make his career a success. Damned hard.

He'd dreamed of being with the FBI since he was a kid.

He'd actually dreamed that his dad was FBI, the job being the reason he'd had to leave his wife and young son. By his teens, he'd come to accept the truth, that his father was simply a deadbeat loser. But the FBI dream had stuck.

It was all he'd ever wanted.

It was all he really was.

And he couldn't give it up. Or do anything further to jeopardize it. Not even to protect the woman he was falling in love with.

The bottom line? He had to choose between his career and Maya.

12

SIMON STRODE THROUGH the town square, looking for Maya's car. They were supposed to meet for lunch, so he'd had the cab drop him off just outside Black Oak. He needed the walking time to think, to strategize.

This was the case of a lifetime. Even now, with multiple people involved and Hunter calling the shots, the bust would still skyrocket Simon's career.

And Maya was the woman of a lifetime. Amazing and sexy. Funny and sweet. Strong, with deep layers of vulnerability that made him wish he were a superhero who could fix all her problems and make her happy. See her smile.

Simon shoved his hands into his pockets and kicked a rock out of his path. Lucky him, getting to choose between two dreams-of-a-lifetime.

Lost in thought, he paused by the statue at the center of the square and took a deep breath. He didn't have answers. He didn't know what he wanted more. So he'd do what he always did when faced with a seemingly insurmountable problem.

He'd wing it.

"Hey, there, big boy."

It wasn't until the greeting was followed by a pat to his ass that Simon realized the woman was talking to him.

"What the…" He spun on his heel to glare. So much for lightning fast reflexes and being in the prime of his career. Thank God he'd chosen his ankle holster over holstering his gun at his back as usual. Now that he was officially on the case, he was armed. But he'd been worried about Maya getting too close.

Apparently he should have been more worried about Lilah.

"Happy New Year," Lilah said, her smile just this side of wicked. "I can't believe you're spending the first day of the year alone. What's up? Did Maya desert you?"

"She's spending the morning with her dad," Simon said. And from the tight look on Lilah's face, she knew that. He had to wonder how Maya's presence had shifted Lilah's cushy position. From what he'd seen at the party the previous night, their relationship was starting to fray a bit. "I'm meeting her at Moonspun Dreams for lunch in about twenty minutes, though."

The friendly look in Lilah's eyes changed. Became more calculating. She glanced over her shoulder toward Pandora's café. When she looked back at Simon, she looked a little harder.

"Okay, fine," she agreed. "You have lunch plans. But you have a little bit of time. How about I show you something?"

He wasn't big on offending women, but this was getting ridiculous.

"I already told you—"

"Not that," she interrupted with an eye roll and a playful swipe at his shoulder. "Tobias finished up a gorgeous custom bike. The tank is airbrushed with a really sexy image over the flag of Texas. You'll love it. The image is my silhouette, naked. And then there's the Texas thing and you being from there and all."

He tried to ignore the naked part of her description and focused on the flag. Baffled, he shook his head. "I'm not from Texas."

"No? But you have the accent and boots. That says cowboy to me."

Right. Because there were no other Southern states. Simon debated. Not about correcting her. That was pointless. But over the invitation.

Gut aching, his muscles tensed as he struggled with a decision he'd secretly been hoping to avoid. If he went with Lilah, he had no idea if it'd lead to a break in the case. If it did, everything would be out in the open. That he wasn't who he'd told Maya. That he wasn't what he'd pretended to be. And that he'd used her in his quest to arrest her father.

In other words, he'd lose Maya.

But Hunter trusted him to do his job. To follow the law he'd sworn to uphold. To give one hundred percent to the job he loved, the career that had forged his identity.

What a freaking choice.

Then again, he realized, now that Hunter was here, the truth was going to come out one way or the other. Eventually, Maya would know he'd lied.

So really, there wasn't any choice.

Miserable, Simon did the only thing he could do. He gestured in the direction of the bike shop and said, "Sure. Let's go see that bike."

He kept a careful eye out, knowing if he caught sight of Maya that he'd abandon the investigation without a second thought.

But luckily, or unluckily, by the time they reached the door of Black Custom Bikes, he hadn't seen even a hint of her, or her car.

"After you," he said with a grimace, holding the door open for Lilah.

"Hey, Jason," she said as she waltzed into the storeroom. "I'll cover now if you want to take your lunch."

The salesman's teeth flashed bright and white as he gave her a knowing look. He slid his gaze to Simon and offered a pitying sort of shake of his head.

"Sure enough. I'll head out for a while. Don't leave the shop unattended, though," he said as he headed for the door.

"He do that often?" Simon wondered. "Just leave the shop in your hands?"

Which would make it extremely convenient for Lilah to use the shop for whatever games she liked. Whether they were sexual, or criminal, Simon still wasn't sure.

Lilah sauntered over and flipped the Open sign to Closed, then locked the door.

"Didn't he ask you to keep the shop open?"

"Nope. He said not to leave it unattended. I'll be attending just fine. But in the back."

He frowned. Time to go. He'd figured on customers, employees, things like that to distract Lilah while he poked around. He had no desire to be in an empty shop with her, though. Especially when she was clearly up to something.

"Oh, look. It's just you and me," she said as she turned a circle with her arms outstretched to indicate the empty room.

The radio in the corner was on, playing Top Forties. The orange light on the coffeepot glowed bright and there was a half-eaten sandwich on the small table in the corner.

Obviously Jason had lied about needing to get lunch.

There were a couple bikes in various states of repair, but nothing sporting a state flag.

"I thought we were here to see a bike," he said, making a show of looking around. But instead of searching for a bike, he was checking for crates, automatic weapons or any other sign of criminal activity that he could report to Hunter.

"Oopsie. It looks like someone's out test-driving the bike."

"Right," he said, since it was clear that she'd known the bike would be gone. He didn't see the crates at first glance either. He strode over to the expanse of windows flanking the back of the shop facing the alley and Pandora's café, and said, "Hey, this is convenient. I can go out this way and meet Maya."

As soon as the words were out, something caught his eye. A large red four-wheel-drive truck all tricked out with shiny chrome was parked at the end of the alley. In the back were at least eight crates, just like the one he'd saw the other day.

Instincts humming, he memorized the license plate number. He knew there were weapons on those crates. And someone was cocky enough to leave them sitting there in the open like that. Hell, even if it were just bike parts, that'd be a pretty dumb move, leaving them out there for anyone to snag.

Which meant whoever it was had to be close by. Probably getting ready to leave. To deliver the guns. Hell, yeah. Excitement surged as Simon realized he could blow this case wide open.

He weighed the options. It'd be a bigger bust, a stronger one, if he could find out where they were taking the weapons. Who they were delivering them to. If he stowed away in that truck, he could find out. Or he could text Hunter and wait for orders. Or, preferably, do both.

Adrenaline zinging, he was ready to rock. He just had to get rid of Lilah.

He turned to ask her if she knew someone who drove a red diesel. As soon as he saw her, though, his jaw dropped and he forgot the question.

"What the hell?"

She was half-naked. Her jacket, shirt and boots were tossed aside so she stood there in unbuttoned jeans and a bra that was putting its elastic to the test.

"You seem to be missing some things," he muttered, cring-

ing as he heard a car engine. Dammit. He didn't have time t
play pawn in her one-upmanship game with Maya. He gav
a quick look out the window again and saw that the truc
hadn't moved. Yet.

When he glanced back, she was five steps closer. How th
hell did she move so fast in those gut-strangling jeans?

"Look," he started. Then he stopped. What did he say
She knew damned well he wasn't interested. So why was sh
half-naked?

"Why are you doing this?" he asked, actually curious be
neath the cringing sort of horror. "Someone could come i
at any moment."

"That just adds a little extra spice to the fun," she said
starting to dance, her arms waving in sinuous moves ove
her head as she undulated her hips. "I like the idea of getting
caught. Of people watching. I like being…naughty."

"That's your idea of naughty?" He thought of Maya's gam
of Simon Says. Now that was naughty. This? This was just..
He eyed Lilah, noting the calculating look in her eyes and th
way she kept shimmying in full view of the windows. Like
she wanted to be seen. He glanced over his shoulder, noting
the unimpeded view from Pandora's café to Lilah's almost-
naked dance.

A dance that plenty of lunchtime patrons were privy to.
Including, at any minute, Maya.

"Clever." He had to hand it to her, if her goal was to sti
up talk, or to piss off Maya, she was playing her hand well.

And she, and the resulting watching crowd, were making
it impossible for him to sneak into the back of the truck. He
was under orders not to break cover, so he couldn't approach
the driver publically. Frustration simmered in his gut. At this
moment, all he could hope for was that someone saw who
was driving.

"What's the problem, big boy?" Lilah purred, doing a

weird sort of shimmy all around him. For all her wiggling her silicon barely jiggled. "You're not man enough to handle me?"

"More like not interested," he told her, sidestepping her next shimmy to shift around her so he was closer to the door. "I'm involved, remember?"

"So what?"

"So? So are you, remember?" He pulled a face. "Don't you think Tobias deserves some kind of loyalty?"

For just a second, her fake sexy look disappeared and a vicious glare took its place. Then she blinked and fluttered her lashes. "Tobias always gets exactly what he deserves. I'm sure he will this time, too. Right now it's all about you and me, big boy."

"I really wish you'd stop calling me big boy."

"Why? Size problems?"

Did she really think that kind of dare was going to make him respond? Almost feeling sorry for her, he just shook his head. "Like I said, I'm involved with Maya. Exclusively."

And he wanted to stay that way. Long after this case was closed, after he'd spilled his guts and shared the truth. Whether that was possible or not, he had no idea. But he was damned sure going to try.

And there was no way in hell he was going to let Lilah mess that up for him.

"Maya doesn't have to know."

Simon smirked. Right. Like everyone watching through the window wouldn't be broadcasting a critique of this show through town faster than he could run from the building.

Impatient and tired of the game, Simon gestured toward her clothes. "Get dressed. I'm not interested, and neither are you."

A loud roar filled the air. A diesel engine, Simon realized.

A tiny smirk flashed on Lilah's face, then she lifted her chin and put on an affronted look.

"You think you can reject me like this? I won't have it. You don't appreciate what I have to offer, then I'll take it somewhere else." She grabbed her jacket and slung it on, then snapped her boots up and stormed for the door.

"You just wait. I'll get revenge for this, Simon. You think your relationship with Little Miss Perfect is so wonderful? Wait until I'm done with it."

With that and a toss of her hair, she was gone.

God, he was an idiot. He'd thought the show was to cause trouble for him and to hurt Maya. But that was just a side benefit. Lilah's way of giving one last swipe at Maya and causing as much trouble as she could for her and Tobias. The real reason, though, had been to keep him distracted, stuck here, so whoever was in the truck could get away.

"Shit." He punched the wall, welcoming the stinging pain as he glared at the doorway where Lilah had stormed through.

She was the decoy. She was silicone deep in this mess. And she'd just kicked his ass, as far as the case was concerned. To say nothing of what she'd done to the possibility of saving his relationship with Maya once the diners broadcast the details of Lilah's striptease.

Anger and frustration simmering at a low boil, Simon paced the cement floor and shoved his hands through his hair. Once again, he was torn between two priorities. Find Maya and try to mitigate the damage. Or bring Hunter up-to-date on the case.

Not ready to wiggle out from between the rock and the hard place, he decided to do both. Grabbing his phone to call Hunter, he headed for the door. Before he could punch a button—or escape—he heard someone coming down the hall.

Lilah, back for more? Fist clenched, he hoped so. He wanted the truth and she had it.

It wasn't Lilah who stepped through the doorway, though.

Nope, coming in within seconds of his girlfriend storming out topless—the timing of which made it an almost sure-thing that he'd witnessed her departure—was Tobias Black.

"Hello, there," Maya's father greeted with a chilly sort of smile. "And what might you be doing here?"

"I've got to go," Simon said impatiently. Torn, he hesitated for a second. Then he went with his gut. "Look, Lilah is trouble. She's trying to cause problems, to hurt Maya. I don't know if plays for you or not, but I figured you should know. Just in case you wanted to put your daughter's needs first or something."

Stepping way over the line there, Simon realized. But he didn't care. Maya needed someone standing up for her.

Tobias gave him a long look. Face inscrutable, the older man glanced at the sweater still strewn across a bike fork, then looked back at Simon.

"Intriguing timing. You and my daughter... Are you planning to make this real?"

How much did Tobias know? Was he speaking as a father, or something else? Simon's instincts screamed.

"Real?" Simon drew the word out, buying time as he tried to read Tobias's expression. But the man hadn't made it to the top of his game by giving anything away. "Is this your way of asking me what my intentions are toward Maya?"

"Sure. Or you could take it as my way of checking on what was going on here?"

Simon's gaze cut to the spot where Lilah had done her little striptease. Wincing, he looked out the window toward the café, wondering how many people were searching for Maya right that second.

"Nothing went on."

"Let me give you a little piece of advice, son. Maya is a strong woman. She's loyal and loving and clever." Waiting for Simon's nod, he continued, "But if you want a future with her—a real future—she needs to know how important she is to you. And you need to realize that she'll forgive anything. As long as there's love—and a heartfelt apology—that goes with your explanation."

"Apologize?" It was like looking down the barrel of a gun without knowing whether it was loaded or not. Was he talking about Lilah's striptease? Or were Simon's instincts right and Tobias knew more than he should about why he and Maya were together? Or worse, about Simon's real job? There were just so many ways for this to explode, it was impossible to know which direction to duck. But one thing was for sure... "You think an apology is going to be necessary? Won't she be okay with a reasonable explanation?"

Tobias laughed in his face.

"Learn from my mistakes, son. That's where I went wrong before. It didn't matter what my explanation was. It didn't matter that I was right, and completely justified and well-motivated in my choices. What mattered was that I never apologized. I expected Maya to accept—unconditionally accept—my explanation. But I forgot to apologize. And I lost her."

For the first time since they met, Tobias looked old. Old and worn and sad.

"Just remember," Tobias continued after clearing his throat, "your secrets aren't so secret. And everything's going to come to a head sooner than later. You'd best figure out your priorities, and decide how you're going to handle the fallout."

Simon felt like a man dancing on hot coals, not sure which way to run. Did he call Tobias's bluff? Did he admit that he and Maya had just met a week ago? That the only reason she'd brought him was to save face with her slutty old school friend?

"Look," he started, not quite sure where he was going but knowing he needed to do some damage control. Before he could say another word, though, there was a loud crash. The far wall shook, a moan echoing through the room. Another bang.

Exchanging shocked looks, the men ran for the door. Simon reached it first, shaking the locked knob.

"Key?" he demanded over his shoulder.

"Don't have one. I didn't even know that door locked," Tobias said, his face drawn tight.

"What's in here?" Simon asked. Then he shook his head. "Doesn't matter. Stand back."

With that warning, he grabbed his gun. He stepped backward, then rammed the door with his shoulder. Pain exploded, but the door didn't budge. He slammed it again.

Wood cracked, sending splinters flying. The door flew open, smacking the wall and ricocheting back.

He rushed into the room, Tobias right on his heels.

A narrow bed and sink spanned the far wall, a set of lockers and a table were tucked under the small window. A door was ajar, muted light from the alley beyond shining through the dust motes.

Facedown on the floor, arm outstretched toward Simon's feet, was a body. Blood oozed from a nasty gash on the back of the man's head.

"Shit." Tobias's curse was low and furious. "That's Jason. My manager. Is he…" His swallow was a loud click, then he sucked in a breath and tried again. "Is he dead?"

Simon hurried across the room. The wound was severe. There were scratches on his arms, too. Careful not to contaminate the scene, he crouched down and took the man's wrist. He had a pulse. Faint, but steady.

"He's alive."

"Thank God."

Simon always did when he was lucky enough to come across a body that survived.

"I need you to get your son. Quickly and quietly. I don't have his direct number and he's going to need to get here fast. You can get him faster than if I call 911."

"Someone is going to pay for this."

Simon glanced up at Tobias's vow. The older man might be green around the gills, but mostly he looked pissed.

"Yep. Someone will. But first we need the sheriff. You get him." He pulled his phone from his pocket, preparing to send a coded text. "I'll take care of the rest."

MAYA WALKED ALONG THE sidewalk toward the sheriff's office lost in thought. Her gait was quick, almost jerky, reflecting the nerves duking it out in her stomach.

She blamed her dad. He'd asked her to meet him after breakfast, then had confused her and made her cry by apologizing. Tobias Black had apologized. That's all it'd taken to melt the last few thin threads of anger she'd been holding on to. What was left?

She had to wait and see.

Which is exactly what she'd said to her dad before she'd left to meet Simon.

Simon. But the last thing she wanted to add was more confusion to her already overstressed emotions. She needed a minute—or a few dozen of them—to figure out what she felt. What she wanted.

And how better to do that than with someone who'd already dealt with the drama of dad and the craziness of falling in love. With a deep breath, she pushed the door of the jail open and strode in.

"Caleb?" she yelled. "It's your fault I'm here so you have to do your big brother thing and help me fix this mess."

She stopped so fast, she almost fell on her face. Shock and embarrassment heated her cheeks as she sucked in a breath and tried to decide if she should turn around and leave, or bluff it out.

"Maya," Caleb said quietly, his tone formal. But his eyes danced with amusement, obviously enjoying her discomfort with brotherly glee. "Can I help you?"

Eyes wide, she glanced at the man sitting across from her brother. Bluff it was.

"I didn't mean to interrupt." In for a penny, in for a pound, if she was going to bluff she was going to do it in style. So she crossed the room, putting just a hint of swing in her hips, and held out her hand. "Hello. I'm Maya. We met last night. You're apparently friends with my boyfriend."

"Hunter." The hand that engulfed hers was hard and sure, just as the man's face was. Just this side of pretty, he had an intensity that made Maya shiver. Maybe it was being at the jail, or something about this man, but all of her instincts screamed *run*. And the only thing that sent that cry through her was a cop. She heard his phone buzz in his pocket, but he ignored it. Instead he kept those dark eyes on her. Judging.

"I know you went to college with Caleb, but what do you do now?" she questioned.

"I'm in securities."

Another form of cop.

"Okay," she murmured, suddenly even more uncomfortable. She crossed her arms over her chest and gave her brother a long look. "Caleb, we need to talk. When will you have a moment?"

His amusement gave away to a slight frown as he inspected her face for some sign of what she wanted. Or more likely, for how much she knew.

Before he could answer, though, the door swung open
Maya shot Caleb a quick glance, noting he looked just as
shocked as she felt.

"Dad?" they said together.

Tobias gave his children a nod of acknowledgement, but
addressed Hunter directly.

"We've got a problem."

13

HORRIFIED, MAYA WRAPPED her arms wrapped around her middle and watched the EMTs load her father's manager into the back of an ambulance.

Someone had tried to kill Jason Raines. She remembered him from school. He was Caleb's age, had spent time hanging with her brother from time to time. Conceited, charming and funny, he'd been a nice guy.

And now he'd had his head bashed in.

"He should be okay," she heard Caleb say. The words were hazy, though, as if coming from a long distance.

And then there was Simon. Looking more comfortable and at ease than she'd ever seen him, he was huddled up with that Hunter guy. Despite being dressed in jeans and jackets, the two of them had an official air that was unmistakable. A red haze of fury fogged her eyes, pushing its way through the misery. Just what, officially, was Simon?

Caleb joined them, and after a quick argument between him and Hunter, he gave Simon a viscous glare. His gaze cut to Maya, meeting her eyes for a brief second. That look sent her stomach tumbling into her toes and her heart racing. Something was wrong.

"You okay, Pumpkin?"

Her eyes met her father's worried gaze. Without thinking she burrowed into his waiting arms.

"I didn't realize you knew Jason that well," he said.

"I didn't."

"Then why..." His words trailed off as his gaze landed on the three men huddled together.

"Ahh. I take it you've met Mr. Hunter?"

"Caleb said they were roommates in college. He left out the rest of what they are."

"Your brother was recruited by the DEA during college. I suppose there were other recruiters visiting his dorm room," Tobias mused.

Something in his voice had Maya lifting her head from the comforting curve of his shoulder to look into his face. "You know what Hunter does?"

Tobias smiled.

"Well?" she prodded.

"This is neither the time, nor the place. Nor, actually, is it my information to share."

She watched Simon take charge of the conversation. Hunter was nodding. Caleb, though still looking furious, finally threw his hands in the air in agreement.

Whatever Hunter did, Simon did, too.

And she was sure what Hunter wasn't, was an investment broker.

Which meant Simon had lied to her.

Had used her.

But why?

He glanced over, his gaze flashing from her to her father, then back. His expression didn't change, but she saw something in his eyes, even from this distance.

Regret.

There was only one reason he'd pretend to be something he wasn't and get her to bring him to her hometown. Only

ne thing in town anyone in law enforcement would be after
n Black Oak.

Her arms tightened protectively around her father's waist.

Her guts clenched, tight and painful in her belly. Simon
ad used her to get to her father? Betrayal left a bitter taste
n her tongue.

"We should go," she whispered through the blood roaring
hrough her head. "Dad, let's go."

His arms tightened, but he wouldn't move.

All of her anger, her petty issues, disappeared.

So he was fallible. And human.

He was still her father.

"Let the game play out, Pumpkin."

"The stakes are too high. You don't know..." Her words
railed off when she glanced at her father's face. Implacable.
And confident. She drew strength from the latter since she
knew she couldn't get past the former.

She vowed to do whatever she could, use whatever she
ad, to mitigate any problems she herself had created by
ringing Simon to town.

As if he could read her mind, he looked over. He said
omething to the other men. Hunter pulled out his cell phone,
ut Caleb glanced their way. Maya tried to read her broth-
r's expression. She tried to take comfort in the hope that he
vouldn't be in on anything that would hurt their father.

Except she knew that Caleb toed firmly to that legal line
e'd chosen when he'd joined the DEA.

Simon said something else and Caleb nodded, then headed
lown the alley. He didn't look back. He didn't stop to talk to
is family. He just left.

Maya's guts turned liquid. Her fingers dug into her fa-
her's jacket so tight, she was pretty sure she could feel his
ibs. Simon headed their way.

"Maya, Mr. Black," he greeted quietly after looking

around at the crowd. His eyes were distant, but alert. He carried an air of violence and authority that she'd never noticed before.

Probably because he'd been lying to her before.

"We're heading to the sheriff's office," he said. His words were for both of them, but his gaze was locked on Maya. "Could the two of you join us?"

"Why Maya?" her father asked.

"Safety."

Her father's arms tightened around her shoulders for one second. Maya almost whimpered when he unwrapped her from his protective hold. He gave her a long look, as if checking to make sure she could deal with whatever was about to happen. Then he gave a nod.

Like he was sure she could handle anything that was coming.

Why, she didn't know. Because she sure as hell wasn't.

"Mr. Black?"

They all turned to face Hunter. He was just as pretty as he'd been before, but now Maya hated him. Hated what he stood for, even though she had no idea what that was.

"Will you walk with me over to the jail? Barton will bring your daughter in a few minutes."

"Why?" Maya snapped. "Why separate us? What are you planning?"

All three men gave her calming looks. Pacify the drama queen? But she wasn't about to be pacified.

"Pumpkin," her father started to say.

"Maya," Simon said at the same time. He didn't touch her. Maybe he knew if he tried, she'd bite him. But his tone was just as calming as the sweep of his fingers down her back would have been. "Someone hurt Jason Raines badly. The EMTs say he'll make it, but only because we found him so quickly. Someone is likely targeting people associated with

Black Custom Bikes, which means you and your father both might be in danger."

"Dad?" she asked, her voice low with fear.

"It's okay, Pumpkin."

"Your brother went to secure his office, to make sure the jail was safe. Hunter will walk your father over, protecting him. Once they're there, we'll follow."

Her father patted her shoulder, then gestured with his chin toward the end of the alley. "Shall we, Mr. Hunter?"

Without a word, Hunter turned and left. The younger man was alert, keeping Tobias one step ahead of him, his hand loose, but poised at his side as if ready to grab a weapon.

"Hunter will text when they're at the jail," Simon said, his tone soothing.

But Maya had no interest in being soothed.

"Who are you?" she demanded. "I mean, really, who are you? You're obviously not an investment pretty boy. And given how chummy you are with Caleb's college roommate, who has a major cop vibe going on, I don't think it's too hard to guess what field you're really in."

Bottle-green eyes stared into hers but all she could see in those gorgeous depths was an apology. Something she had no interest in. All she wanted from him was the truth.

"Maya—"

"I don't want to hear any of your bullshit," she warned in a low growl. Stepping toe to toe, she poked her finger into his chest in a single sharp jab and glared. "You lied to me before. Now I want the truth."

The conflict on his face was almost as painful for her to see as it obviously was for him to experience. He grimaced, then reached out to take her hand. Not wanting him touching her, Maya tried to pull away. But he wouldn't let go.

"Look, I don't want to hurt you. Whatever else you believe, please know that's the truth."

She gave him her *whatever* look.

"I promise, I'll explain everything," he told her. He shot a quick look around the crowd, then took a deep breath as if he were making a major decision. Before he could act on it, though, his cell phone buzzed.

He glanced at the display. His jaw stiffened like he was clenching his teeth. Then he shoved the phone back in his pocket and looked at Maya.

"Let's go."

"Not until you explain everything."

"Explanations are waiting at your brother's office."

"I want to hear them from you. Now."

He gave her a long look. Like she'd just asked him to choose between cutting off his arm, or his leg. Then he gave a slow, regretful shake of his head. "Let's go."

Maya gritted her teeth so hard, she was surprised they didn't crack. Then she puffed out a breath and lifted her own chin. "Fine. But you and I? We're not finished with this."

He tried to put his arm around her shoulder but she shrugged him off. One hand under his jacket, most likely on a gun, he finally settled for taking her arm. She thought about yanking free but the warning look he gave her made her think twice.

Their walk was eventless. People stared, a few pointed, but other than the anger mounting with each stamp of Maya's feet, nothing happened.

Releasing her arm, Simon opened the door to the jailhouse and gestured for her to precede him. Her father, brother and Hunter were already there. Caleb behind his desk looking all official. Hunter leaning against a wall, observing. And Tobias pouring himself a cup of coffee, looking oddly smug given the enormity of the circumstances.

"Now that we're all here, we can work together to get to the bottom of this situation," Hunter said, instantly taking command of the room. "According to the report I've received, there is a cache of weapons being ran through Black Custom Bikes. After receiving this information, I ran checks on all of Tobias's employees and associates."

Maya gasped, her worried eyes cutting to her father. He didn't look concerned, though. Why was he not freaking out?

"Before we get into that, why don't you tell me where you got that report," Caleb interrupted, his face hard with anger. "I might be new at this sheriffing gig, but I'm pretty damned sure that should have been run past me."

"I'm running it all past you now," Hunter said, his words calm and assured.

"Who filed the report?" Caleb prodded.

For the first time since she'd met him, Hunter looked uncomfortable. He gave her an odd look, then inclined his head toward Simon.

"Simon?" Maya whispered. *No! Please, no.* Don't let him have betrayed her. She knew it was a useless plea. Because her gut—her heart—knew he had.

She stared at him with devastated eyes. After a nod from Hunter, Simon cleared his throat and reported, "Three days ago I uncovered a cache of fully automatic lower receivers being ran through Black Custom Bikes. We ascertained by running the serial number that the weapons were meant for a military facility in Texas and were reported stolen a month ago."

"You think my father stole illegal guns?" Maya asked in horror. She'd suspected it, but hearing proof was like a kick in the gut. Maya was horrified. Not only that she'd brought him here, but that she'd freaking paid him to come.

Which was worse? His betrayal of her? Or her betrayal of her father? Tears gathered, hot and aching, behind her eyes. But Maya refused to let them fall. There was no way she'd let Simon know how much he'd hurt her.

"WE DON'T THINK YOUR father stole the guns," Simon insiste•
just a second before Hunter echoed his denial.

He couldn't stand to see Maya so upset. God, this sucked
He'd spent the past twenty-four hours mentally tossing an•
turning between her and his career. But now when faced witl
the results of his inadvertent choice, he knew he'd made th•
wrong one. Maya should have come first.

"We think someone is using your father's shop as a ship
ping point, hiding the weapons in crates of motorcycle parts,"
Hunter explained. "Since this is the second setup in as many
months, it's clear someone is trying to set him up for an ugl•
fall."

"Lilah was involved in this, wasn't she?" Tobias asked
His tone more than his words made Simon turn and face th•
man he'd spent his entire career hoping to arrest. He looke•
as ashamedly angry as he sounded. "I was so focused o•
using her to get Maya home, I missed the signs that she wa•
using me as well."

Simon winced. Meeting Hunter's insistent gaze, he sighe•
and, obeying the unspoken order, stepped forward.

"It wasn't Lilah."

"How do you know?" Caleb asked.

"She has an alibi."

Simon wanted nothing more than five minutes alone witl
Maya. A chance to explain. To take Tobias's advice and te•
her how sorry he was.

He didn't care about his promotion. He didn't even car•
about his career. In this second, right now, he'd walk awa•
from it all if it meant keeping Maya.

But that wasn't his choice to make.

And from the look on her face, so coldly defensive an•
angry, their future had ended about ten minutes ago.

So he kissed happiness goodbye and continued with hi•
report.

"Because in the time leading up to Jason Raines getting whacked over the head, Lilah Gomez was with me."

"With you," Caleb repeated. His face looked like it was carved in stone. Very angry, potentially violent stone.

"Stripping down to her underwear while she danced around the shop in the back of Black Custom Bikes. There are plenty of witnesses, since she was doing it right in front of the windows and the customers at Moonspun Dreams were in the audience."

"Stripping."

Simon glowered at Caleb, wishing the man would quit repeating everything he said. It wasn't like Maya had missed the declaration the first time. Her teary-eyed glare made that abundantly clear.

"I didn't ask her to, and had no interest in the show."

Then, because he needed to get this over with so he could attempt to save the best thing that'd ever happened to him, he focused exclusively on Hunter. Just giving a report. No betrayal here, no expectations. Just the job.

"She was there from eleven-fifteen until eleven-twenty-seven. It's been established that the victim was hit at approximately eleven-thirty. The attacker entered through the side door. It's not clearly visible from Moonspun Dreams' windows. Witnesses saw Jason Raines come around the building, pause for a conversation with Lucas, the mechanic, before Lucas drove off in the company truck to make deliveries. However, nobody interviewed saw anyone else coming or going."

Unable to stop himself, Simon's gaze cut to Maya for a brief second. Her lower lip trembling, she stared at him through betrayed eyes.

Damning himself, he forced himself to continue his report.

"Caleb has ascertained that there's no way anyone could get from the front entrance of Black Custom Bikes down three businesses to the end of the sidewalk and around to the side door in less than five minutes. Whether she's connected in some other way or not, Lilah Gomez is alibied for the actual assault."

"Did you establish motive for her visit?" Hunter queried, his face expressionless as usual. "Other than her apparent desire to put on a show, that is."

"The show was just that, a show, sir. While I have no doubt she'd have accepted an advance, my impression was that she had a more specific reason for her visit." This time he didn't let himself look toward Maya. He could hear her breath, shaky and rough, and knew she was crying. His gut clenched. He was the world's biggest jerk.

"Barton."

Hunter's reminder pulled him back. With a grimace, Simon reluctantly continued. "From what I've been able to discern in my investigation over the past few days, Lilah Gomez's primary goal is to extort as much money as possible from Black Custom Bikes. She's promising customers favors, special deals and sneaking added features on to their orders in exchange for cash in her pocket."

He glanced over at Tobias, noting that the older man didn't look surprised. Did the guy know everything that was going on, and if so, why was Hunter even here?

"She's…" Regardless of how much Tobias knew, screwing just sounded tacky. "She's having an *affair* with Jason Raines. She made like she wanted to start something hot with me, but that was mostly theater."

"Theater, my ass," Maya muttered.

Bracing himself, Simon looked at her. Hair a little wild from shoving her fingers through it and her face tearstained beneath the fury, she was curled into her brother's arms.

"I'm not saying she wouldn't have given the opportunity,

out I wasn't interested in offering her a chance. And since sex wasn't her actual motivation, she wasn't pushing the issue."

He winced at the watery snort of disbelief coming from Maya's corner of the room.

"What was her real motivation?" Caleb asked, sounding like he believed not one word of Simon's report.

"To hurt Maya," Simon said simply.

Before anyone could react, the phone rang. Caleb released his sister to stride over and grab it.

"Black," he answered.

Listening, his brow furrowed and he shot a glance toward Hunter.

"You're sure?" He grimaced, then added, "Fine. Bring her in."

Hanging up, he said, "That was the state police. They picked up the truck Barton I.D.'d. Lucas claims he's making deliveries. They counted the crates. Same number Barton reported were loaded in the bed of the truck. They didn't find any weapons."

"Do you have an APB out on Lilah?" Hunter asked.

Stone-faced, Caleb nodded.

"She's clearly involved," Simon agreed. "But she's not the mastermind. This is a carefully orchestrated ring. The drugs last month, now guns. There's something bigger going on."

Hunter nodded and Caleb jerked his head in agreement. Tobias looked resigned, but not surprised. Only Maya seemed upset.

"A crime ring? Apparently one that's targeting my father." She bypassed her brother to stomp over to Hunter and glare into his face. "What are you doing about this?"

"What am *I* doing?" Hunter actually looked shocked.

"Yes, you. You're obviously in charge. What the hell are you doing to protect my father? To keep his good name from being dirtied by this ugly mess?"

Good name?

Caleb snorted so hard he almost knocked over his coffee.
Even Tobias looked surprised at that declaration. Simon
couldn't hold back his own grin.

He had to hand it to Hunter, though. The guy didn't even
blink. Instead he gave Maya a look that was somewhere be
tween sympathy and warning. "Ms. Black, I assure you
we've got this under control. Your father isn't under suspi
cion, nor is he in danger."

"We? Who the hell is *we?*" she demanded. Before Hunter
could respond, she spun around and pointed at Simon.
"You're a part of his *we.* So you tell me. Who do you work
for?"

Simon cut a glance at Hunter and got the go ahead. He
steeled himself, then told her, "FBI."

As if someone had poked a sharp pin in Maya's balloon of
angry energy, she simply deflated. Her shoulders drooped,
her eyes filled with fear and she seemed to shrink. "FBI?"
she whispered. "You used me. From the beginning. You lied
about everything."

"Not everything," Simon protested. Then he stopped
shaking his head in regret. She was right. He had no de
fense. All he could do was take Tobias's advice. "Maya, I'm
sorry. I can explain everything, try and justify my choices.
But none of that changes the fact that I hurt you."

She gave him a long, indecipherable look. Then she
stepped away.

"You hurt me, and you used me to hurt people I care about.
You and I? We are through," she told him, her words causing
an actual pain in his heart. "Completely."

With that and one last glare, she turned on her heel and
stormed out the door.

Simon wanted to run after her, but he knew it was point
less. Hunter inclined his head to indicate that he had some

one outside by now, ready to follow her and make sure she was safe.

"Son, you have some work ahead of you."

Startled, he looked at Tobias. He'd been so caught up in having his heart ripped from his chest, he'd forgotten the other men were there.

"Work?"

All three nodded.

"On the case?"

They gave him pitying looks.

His gaze went to the door and he sighed and shook his head.

"No point. That particular case is clearly closed."

Caleb looked smug. Hunter's face was impassive, as usual, but there was a hint of sympathy in his eyes. And Tobias? He was grinning. Why? Some instinct told him that Simon's main objective had been to bust him, and this was his revenge?

"I'm gonna do you boys a favor," Tobias said expansively, taking a seat behind the desk, propping his feet up and leaning back in the chair with a wicked sort of look on his face. "I'm gonna tell you how to handle women."

"Dad—"

"Don't interrupt, Caleb. You might be sitting pretty with that sweet Pandora right now, but you're going to need this information at some point. This, or a surefire method of groveling."

Caleb's brows shot up. He and Simon exchanged a look, then he plopped his butt on the other desk with a shrug and waited.

Apparently they were about to learn the ways of women from a master con artist.

Simon was so desperate, it was all he could do not to pull out his notepad and pen so he didn't miss anything.

"The key to handling women is to ask yourself one single question," Tobias instructed. "Do you care? If you do, you'll do whatever it takes to make them happy. And if you don't, just walk away. There's no point in wasting your time."

"That's it?" Caleb asked.

"That's it," his father confirmed.

Caleb laughed. But Simon leaned back with a sigh. Simple, yes. But the wisdom of those words was unmistakable.

He definitely cared enough. Now he just had to figure out what it would take to make Maya happy.

14

MAYA CURLED UP ON THE bed with her laptop while Dottie rubbed her sweet furry head against her shoulder. She'd been comforted by the cat, by her old bedroom and by her dad's cooking for the past two days.

She'd walked out of the sheriff's office and went straight home. It'd been pure instinct. And once she'd gotten here, she'd curled up in her room and let Pandora go to the manor for her and gather her belongings. That'd been pure chicken shit.

But chicken shit avoidance was all she had left.

She'd thought they were falling in love. She'd never felt as safe, as wanted, as she did with Simon. To see him again, knowing he didn't feel any of that for her, it'd hurt too much. Way, way too much.

"It's easier to avoid Simon if I hide here," she told Dottie miserably. The cat purred her agreement. That was the good thing about cats, they weren't judgmental.

Not that she was avoiding him altogether. She'd had a grand ole time hacking into the FBI employee records. Sure, hacking the FBI had been a challenge, but she'd been too upset to sleep the night before. Always mindful of her father's warning about greed, she hadn't poked into anything except Simon's file.

Simon really was his first name, Barton his last. Harris was his mother's maiden name. That'd made things easier. And, oddly enough, most of what he'd told her about himself was true, too. His age, his family history.

She peered at the screen and read his resume. It claimed he spoke three languages, had a photographic memory for numbers and was versed in a multitude of weapons. She hadn't been able to break past the basics to see what kind of work he actually did, though.

Yet.

He'd used her.

There was no getting around that fact.

Of course, she'd used him, too.

"I'm trying to be mad at him, Dottie, but I'm just as guilty as he is. That makes it a lot harder to heat up the mad."

Torn in a million directions, Maya pushed the laptop aside, then shoved both hands through her hair. Guilt was at the forefront, but anger was coming in a close second.

She'd used him to save face—she hadn't wanted to come home alone. And yes, maybe she'd hoped he'd distract Lilah.

But he'd come because he'd hoped to arrest her father.

She'd left her hometown, left her family and changed her name to avoid the connection with her father and his criminal choices.

And Simon? He'd used her for that connection.

There. Finally, anger was drowning out the pain of imagining the rest of her life without him.

Before she could decide whether to fan the flames or try and tone her fury down, there was a quick rap on her door. She didn't have time to do more than glance over before it swung open.

"Hey," Simon said, standing in the doorway. He glanced

behind him, then stepped in and shut the door like he was aiming for privacy.

Her heart racing, Maya scrambled to her knees, glaring first at him, then at the closed door. What? He thought he could just waltz in here and pretend nothing had happed? That everything was hunky-dory between them?

"I didn't invite you into my bedroom," she challenged, trying tried to pretend she wasn't melting at the sight of his gorgeous face. How ridiculous was it that she'd missed him like crazy in the day they'd been separated?

"I needed to talk to you."

Maya lifted her chin in a silent dare for him to go right ahead.

He didn't say anything at first, though. Instead, he walked over to pet the cat. Dottie, the traitor, purred and pushed into his hand instead of attacking as was her wont.

When his elbow knocked into the laptop, it shifted on the bed and pulled out of the sleep mode. He gave the screen an absent glance. Then he looked closer. Even as she told herself she didn't care, Maya cringed a little.

Simon started laughing. A chuckle at first, then he threw back his head in a full-belly laugh.

Fear gone, Maya glared.

"What's so funny?"

"Turnabout's fair play, I suppose," he acknowledged, waving his hand at his onscreen resume. "I have to admit, I'm impressed, too. I didn't realize you were this skilled at hacking."

"I'm sure you checked my criminal record. You knew I'd been arrested for computer invasion," she snapped, humiliated that he'd known her history, both good and bad, from the beginning. He knew all her negatives, while she'd been in awe of his positives.

"You weren't convicted," he reminded her. As if that said it all.

She felt herself melt a little more. She wanted nothing more than to step around the bed—or dive across it—and cuddle into his arms.

"Why are you here, again?" she asked, crossing her arms tight to keep herself from moving.

"We'd planned to leave today, remember? To head home."

"You'll have to find your own way home. I'm not going back to San Francisco," she dismissed with a jerk of her shoulder. "Not yet. Maybe not at all."

He looked a little worried at that. Why? It wasn't like he cared where she ended up.

"What about your job?"

She didn't know. She hadn't figured it all out yet. She just knew she couldn't go back to living the lie of an average life.

"What about your job, Simon? What, exactly, is it that you do for the FBI? Or is lying to gullible women your specialty?" She arched a brow and gave him a thorough once over. She tried to ignore the intense and needy lust she felt at the sight of his long, hard body.

Harder to ignore was how much she loved him.

But she could damned well try.

"Shouldn't you be off playing FBI hero? Finding whoever it is that's trying to hurt my father?"

"I'm working on it," he assured her. "After talking with Lucas, we have a little more information than before."

"Do you know who bashed Jason's head in?"

Simon grimaced. "Not yet. But Lucas was able to provide a list of all his delivery locations. Although we haven't made any arrests, we have recovered the stolen weapons."

"Has Jason confessed? Or provided any information at all?" She'd been asking her brother and Caleb that same question every few hours for the past two days, but neither would tell her anything. "And what about Lilah? She's guilty, too, right?"

Simon nodded. "The state police picked her up an hour ago. She claims she doesn't know who was actually calling the shots. She was approached by Jason after she started dating your dad, so he's the only one she had any contact with. Apparently he told her that whoever is behind the crime ring is someone in power in town, though."

"Someone in power?" Suddenly her excuse to avoid the emotional discussion turned all too serious. Eyes huge, Maya tried to process that. Black Oak wasn't a large town. There were only a handful of people who could be termed movers or shakers. The top of the list, of course, was still her father. "Did she try and blame dad?"

Simon quickly shook his head. "No, your dad's clear. We're keeping that under wraps, though. Hunter doesn't want to tip his hand."

"Are you supposed to be sharing this with me?" she asked slowly.

"Nope. Officially, this is all confidential. But Hunter knows I'm filling you in on the basics."

"And he's okay with that?" Somehow she doubted it. Hunter didn't strike her as the kind of guy to throw rules and regs out the window.

"Let's just say he's waiting to see how I want to handle things before he starts sanctioning me."

His voice deepened, giving a husky edge to that sweet Southern accent. The look he gave her made Maya want to melt all over his feet and forgive him for anything. But she'd gone that route already in her life, until her father had disappointed her one too many times. She couldn't do it again. Not even with someone she loved as much as Simon.

Those damned ever-present tears welled again. Needing

him to leave so she could fall apart in private, Maya waved her hand toward the door.

"If *things* refers to me, then you have nothing to handle. We're finished."

SIMON WINCED AT THE misery on Maya's face. So this was what it felt like to have your heart break. Kinda like getting kicked in the nuts so hard, you knew those poor damaged suckers would never work again.

Desperation surged. His thoughts raced as his brain tried to find a solution that would keep his chance at happiness from slipping off the edge of his fingertips.

She was who he wanted to spend his life with. What he hadn't even realized he was searching for until he'd found her. She was the answer to that empty void that not even career highs and blinding ambition could fill.

There was no way in hell he was letting her go.

No way he was letting Maya go.

Determined, he strode around the bed, braving the unpredictable attack-cat guarding her mistress, and reached for Maya.

"We're not finished," he insisted, turning her to face him. "We need to settle this."

"We're settled," she said with a wobbly lift of her chin. "You're not undercover anymore, so you don't need me. And I definitely don't need you. We're over."

"What if I don't want us to be over?" Terrified that he just might beg, Simon gave in to the desperation that'd been clawing at him. He gripped her shoulders and looked into her golden eyes, then gave in to the need and pulled her tight against him.

Before she could gasp, he took her mouth in a wildly out-of-control kiss. Technique, skill, hell even class, they all flew out the window as he gave in to the worry clawing at his gut.

He was about to lose Maya, and the thought of that made him want to howl and beat his fists against a wall.

Then she kissed him back. Fingers digging sharply into his shoulders, she gave a low moan of surrender.

"Take me," she whispered. "One last time."

So he did.

Fabric ripped as he tugged and pulled her clothes out of his way. His mouth sped over her body, fingers plunged. Her delighted gasps echoed as her own hands clenched his ass, pulling him tighter against her undulating body.

Need pounded through him, passion a distant second. They fell onto the bed together, wrapping around each other as if they were terrified of letting go. Their tongues dueled, fingers urging each other higher, stroking the flames to an unbearable level. He shoved his jeans aside, yanked on a condom.

And plunged.

Maya gave a keening gasp, then a long, delighted moan. Her head fell back, exposing her neck to his questing mouth as she was swept away by an orgasm so strong it shook her body. He plunged once more, then twice.

Then he exploded. His entire body flashed hot as wave after wave of pleasure poured through him. Maya's body milked every last ounce, making him want to come again, a million times over. God, she was incredible.

Then he came back to earth.

His face buried in the curve of her neck, Simon tried to calm his breathing. Had he blown it? Instead of an apology and a few sweet words to persuade Maya to give him another chance, he'd ripped her clothes off and thrown her on the bed. His body was still shaking from the aftershocks of the best orgasm of his life, so he couldn't quite regret the sex. But he sure as hell regretted not winning her over first.

Because sex like this? It should be a prelude to something

bigger. Something special that'd last a lifetime. His heart, still racing, sank to his feet as he gave in to despair.

It shouldn't be a freaking goodbye.

PANTING, MAYA SLOWLY floated back to earth. Her head was spinning. Her heart was racing. And she felt incredible.

"That was just sex," she said breathlessly.

"Bullshit," Simon murmured, his words muffled because his face was still buried in the curve of her neck. "That was proof."

"Proof?" Knowing she wasn't going to find control lying naked under his body, Maya pressed her hands against Simon's shoulders. He instantly rolled away. As soon as his body was clear, she jumped off the bed.

And almost fell on her ass since her leggings were still tangled around her ankles. With a quick tug she pulled them into place and adjusted her shirt.

"Proof of what? That we're good at sex? That we can drive each other crazy wild with just a look? That the orgasms are the best either of us has ever had? So what? That doesn't mean anything."

Simon didn't get up. Instead he shifted onto his back and lay, spread eagle, on the bed. The grin on his face should have made her want to hit him. But instead, it was all Maya could do to keep from giggling.

"Babe, we're not good at sex. We're freaking fantastic." He opened his beautiful green eyes and gave her a long look. "And you wanna know why we're freaking fantastic?"

Her daddy hadn't raised no fools, so Maya knew perfectly well the question was a trap. And yet, she couldn't resist asking, "Why?"

"Because we're in love."

She almost fell to the floor. Her eyes rounded in shock,

he shook her head. He didn't couldn't love her. And even if
e did, she couldn't let it matter.

Because he was just like her father.

Charming, clever and way too good at lying and keeping
ecrets. How could she trust that?

"Admit it," he said, jackknifing upright with an admirable
how of those sexy ab muscles. "We're great together. And
vhen two people are this great, they owe it to themselves to
e together as much as possible."

The mellow glow from hot sex faded. Maya had spent most
f her life living in one big question mark, not sure what new
rick her father would get up to, whether he'd be arrested or
urt. She'd spent the past few years of her life hiding from
er own past and pretending she didn't have her father's blood
unning through her veins.

But now? Now she knew better. She was big enough to
ake care of herself, and to let her father take care of himself,
oo. And she was tired of running and hiding.

From her past.

From her life.

And from herself.

And if she let Simon go, she'd be doing all of that again.

Why? For revenge? To protect herself?

No.

It'd be because she was scared.

And she'd be damned if she'd let go of the man of her
lreams because she was too afraid of her own emotions.

"What do you want to do, Maya?" he asked quietly.

"I'm staying here," she decided. As soon as the words
vere out, she knew they were right. Relief poured through
ler so fast she almost sagged with the intensity. "This is the
ight place for me. I've missed it. I don't know that I'll stay
or good, but for the next little while I'm going to hang out.
'igure out what I want to do next."

"And protect your dad under the guise of reconnectin with your family?"

Maya gave a sheepish little shrug. "Yeah, pretty much. can use Caleb's wedding as reason enough for now. They' set a date for Valentine's Day. That's just over a month away

"You know there's someone in town, probably more tha one someone, with some really bad plans, right?" he ca tioned. Maya frowned, but before she could ask, he shoo his head. "I don't know what they are. But this has the mal ings of something huge coming together. And probably soo Hunter's pretty tense. He knows a lot more than he's sharing

"Are you telling me not to stay?" she asked quietly.

"Would you listen if I did?"

"No," she said, her tone apologetic. "I can't run anymore

"I didn't think so." He didn't sound upset, though. But h did suddenly look really nervous. Maya's stomach tightene in response as she waited. What was he going to do? Whe would he be? What about them?

But Simon didn't say anything. Instead he kept looking her with an intense, almost scary sort of look on his face.

"What are you going to do now?" she asked, needing t know.

"I have a couple of choices. I can be officially assigned t this case and in Black Oak for the next little while."

Joy raced fear in Maya's belly, both flying at speeds tha were only adding to her nervous nausea. But she had to asl "Or?"

"Or I can go back to San Francisco. Get assigned to a office there and make it my new home base."

The ringing in her ears drowned out all sounds excep his voice. Her eyes feasted on his face, trying to read ever nuance. "And what will you decide?"

"Actually, it's what will *you* decide," he said, steppin forward to take both of her hands in his. "I want to be wit you. Wherever you are. Here, San Francisco, Timbuktu. You choose, I'll follow."

"I thought your career was your whole life," she protested. "Even when you were pretending it was investments, the rest was true. I could tell. It's been everything, shaped everything, that's made you who you are."

He nodded. Then he lifted one of her hands to his lips and brushed a soft kiss over her knuckle.

"That's true. It was my whole life. But that was before."

"Before?"

"Before you. Before us." He lifted the other hand, kissing it, then held them both to his chest. "I've finally found something worth living for, Maya. Something worth coming home to, worth hoping for and planning a future around."

She couldn't breathe. Was he saying what it sounded like? A part of her wanted to jump up and down. Another part of her wanted to run from the room before he could finish.

Refusing to look like a chicken, barely able to hear through the blood roaring in her ears, Maya waited.

"Us," he said.

Oh, wow. He'd said the magic word. Everything in her life just took on a shiny glow; the word *us* had sprinkled a glitter of joy over her entire existence.

And oh, God, she was turning into a sap. Maya pressed her lips together, trying to stop the tears that had filled her eyes from spilling over. No way she was going to blubber through something this important.

"Us? Like us for play? Or us for keeps?" She watched his face carefully, looking for signs of desperation or fear. Or even hesitation. But he looked happy. Thrilled, even. Like this was something he really, really wanted.

Like *she* was someone he really, really wanted.

Forever.

"I want to give us a chance at forever," he said quietly,

his mouth brushing over the knuckles of one hand, then the other. "I want to see what it's like when we're both on the same page. Both of us being ourselves, you know."

"Ourselves?"

"I'm in love with you, Maya. But I know you. If we don't spend some time as ourselves, being totally honest and not pretending, you might start doubting this. Thinking we're not solid. I think we need to give it time. I want you to be sure of me. Of us."

He cleared his throat.

"But before you decide anything, you need to know that I'm sorry. I can give you a million excuses as to why I lied, why I used you. But they don't matter. What matters is that I hurt you. And no excuse in the world justifies that."

Maya pulled back a little, her eyes rounding in shock. He really did know her. That last, tiny bit of worry that'd been lurking in the back of her head disappeared.

She wrapped her hands tighter around the back of his neck and pulled Simon's head down for a kiss.

"I'm in love with you, too," she said softly, smiling up at the most beautiful eyes she'd ever seen. "And I think time is a great idea. That way I have longer to prove to you how I feel."

"To say nothing of time to have plenty of hot, wild sex," he said with a grin.

"Oh, yeah," she breathed with a huge sigh, more content and happy than she'd ever thought possible. "We should get started on that right now."

* * * * *

PASSION

For a spicier, decidedly hotter read—
this is your destination for romance!

COMING NEXT MONTH
AVAILABLE JANUARY 31, 2012

#663 ONCE UPON A VALENTINE
Bedtime Stories
Stephanie Bond, Leslie Kelly, Michelle Rowen

#664 THE KEEPER
Men Out of Uniform
Rhonda Nelson

#665 CHOOSE ME
It's Trading Men!
Jo Leigh

#666 SEX, LIES AND VALENTINES
Undercover Operatives
Tawny Weber

#667 BRING IT ON
Island Nights
Kira Sinclair

#668 THE PLAYER'S CLUB: LINCOLN
The Player's Club
Cathy Yardley

REQUEST YOUR FREE BOOKS!
2 FREE NOVELS PLUS 2 FREE GIFTS!

red-hot reads!

YES! Please send me 2 FREE Harlequin® Blaze™ novels and my 2 FREE gifts (gifts are worth about $10). After receiving them, if I don't wish to receive any more books, I can return the shipping statement marked "cancel." If I don't cancel, I will receive 6 brand-new novels every month and be billed just $4.49 per book in the U.S. or $4.96 per book in Canada. That's a saving of at least 14% off the cover price. It's quite a bargain. Shipping and handling is just 50¢ per book in the U.S. and 75¢ per book in Canada.* I understand that accepting the 2 free books and gifts places me under no obligation to buy anything. I can always return a shipment and cancel at any time. Even if I never buy another book, the two free books and gifts are mine to keep forever.

151/351 HDN FEQE

Name	(PLEASE PRINT)

Address	Apt. #

City	State/Prov.	Zip/Postal Code

Signature (if under 18, a parent or guardian must sign)

Mail to the Reader Service:
IN U.S.A.: P.O. Box 1867, Buffalo, NY 14240-1867
IN CANADA: P.O. Box 609, Fort Erie, Ontario L2A 5X3

Not valid for current subscribers to Harlequin Blaze books.

Want to try two free books from another line?
Call 1-800-873-8635 or visit www.ReaderService.com.

* Terms and prices subject to change without notice. Prices do not include applicable taxes. Sales tax applicable in N.Y. Canadian residents will be charged applicable taxes. Offer not valid in Quebec. This offer is limited to one order per household. All orders subject to credit approval. Credit or debit balances in a customer's account(s) may be offset by any other outstanding balance owed by or to the customer. Please allow 4 to 6 weeks for delivery. Offer available while quantities last.

Your Privacy—The Reader Service is committed to protecting your privacy. Our Privacy Policy is available online at www.ReaderService.com or upon request from the Reader Service.

We make a portion of our mailing list available to reputable third parties that offer products we believe may interest you. If you prefer that we not exchange your name with third parties, or if you wish to clarify or modify your communication preferences, please visit us at www.ReaderService.com/consumerschoice or write to us at Reader Service Preference Service, P.O. Box 9062, Buffalo, NY 14269. Include your complete name and address.

HBI1B

Rhonda Nelson

SIZZLES WITH ANOTHER INSTALLMENT OF

When former ranger Jack Martin is assigned to
provide security to Mariette Levine, a local pastry
chef, he believes this will be an open-and-shut case.
Yet the danger becomes all too real when Mariette is
attacked. But things aren't always what they seem,
and soon Jack's protective instincts demand he save
the woman he is quickly falling for.

THE KEEPER

**Available February 2012
wherever books are sold.**

Louisa Morgan loves being around children.
So when she has the opportunity to tutor bedridden Ellie,
she's determined to bring joy back into the motherless
girl's world. Can she also help Ellie's father open his
heart again? Read on for a sneak peek of

THE COWBOY FATHER

by Linda Ford,
available February 2012 from Love Inspired Historical.

Why had Louisa thought she could do this job? A bubble of self-pity whispered she was totally useless, but Louisa ignored it. She wasn't useless. She could help Ellie if the child allowed it.

Emmet walked her out, waiting until they were out of earshot to speak. "I sense you and Ellie are not getting along."

"Ellie has lost her freedom. On top of that, everything is new. Familiar things are gone. Her only defense is to exert what little independence she has left. I believe she will soon tire of it and find there are more enjoyable ways to pass the time."

He looked doubtful. Louisa feared he would tell her not to return. But after several seconds' consideration, he sighed heavily. "You're right about one thing. She's lost everything. She can hardly be blamed for feeling out of sorts."

"She hasn't lost everything, though." Her words were quiet, coming from a place full of certainty that Emmet was more than enough for this child. "She has you."

"She'll always have me. As long as I live." He clenched his fists. "And I fully intend to raise her in such a way that even if something happened to me, she would never feel like I was gone. I'd be in her thoughts and in her actions every day."

Peace filled Louisa. "Exactly what my father did."

Their gazes connected, forged a single thought about fathers and daughters…how each needed the other. How sweet the relationship was.

Louisa tipped her head away first. "I'll see you tomorrow."

Emmet nodded. "Until tomorrow then."

She climbed behind the wheel of their automobile and turned toward home. She admired Emmet's devotion to his child. It reminded her of the love her own father had lavished on Louisa and her sisters. Louisa smiled as fond memories of her father filled her thoughts. Ellie was a fortunate child to know such love.

Louisa understands what both father and daughter are going through. Will her compassion help them heal—and form a new family? Find out in
THE COWBOY FATHER
by Linda Ford, available February 14, 2012.

Love Inspired Books celebrates 15 years of inspirational romance in 2012! February puts the spotlight on Love Inspired Historical, with each book celebrating family and the special place it has in our hearts. Be sure to pick up all four Love Inspired Historical stories, available February 14, wherever books are sold.